ChangelingPress.com

Sting/Deadeye Duet
A Bones MC Romance
Marteeka Karland

Sting/Deadeye Duet
A Bones MC Romance
Marteeka Karland

All rights reserved.
Copyright ©2023 Marteeka Karland

ISBN: 978-1-60521-872-4

Publisher:
Changeling Press LLC
315 N. Centre St.
Martinsburg, WV 25404
ChangelingPress.com

Printed in the U.S.A.

Editor: Katriena Knights
Cover Artist: Marteeka Karland

The individual stories in this anthology have been previously released in E-Book format.

No part of this publication may be reproduced or shared by any electronic or mechanical means, including but not limited to reprinting, photocopying, or digital reproduction, without prior written permission from Changeling Press LLC.

This book contains sexually explicit scenes and adult language which some may find offensive and which is not appropriate for a young audience. Changeling Press books are for sale to adults, only, as defined by the laws of the country in which you made your purchase.

Table of Contents

Sting (Iron Tzars MC 1) 4
   Chapter One 5
   Chapter Two 26
   Chapter Three 39
   Chapter Four 52
   Chapter Five 64
   Chapter Six 80
   Chapter Seven 100
Deadeye (Bones MC 13) 111
   Chapter One 112
   Chapter Two 128
   Chapter Three 141
   Chapter Four 159
   Chapter Five 176
   Chapter Six 193
   Chapter Seven 203
   Chapter Eight 218
Marteeka Karland 226
Changeling Press E-Books 227

Sting (Iron Tzars MC 1)
A Bones MC Romance
Marteeka Karland

Iris -- Since my mother died, my only goal has been to get custody of my sister Jerrica and keep her safe. I was on my way, too -- getting emancipated by the court so I could get a job and prove I had the means to take responsibility for my little sister. I was with her every day until I came to her group home one morning to find she'd been adopted out overnight. It looks like Jerrica is gone from my life forever, but I've got one more trick up my sleeve. Jerrica made friends with a woman from a local motorcycle club. What I didn't count on is *him*. *Sting*. President of Iron Tzars MC. He doesn't know it yet, but once I get Jerrica back, he's next on my list.

Sting -- I wasn't ready to be president of an MC like Iron Tzars, but my father left me little choice. But my daddy taught me well. I tolerate no disloyalty or disrespect and always, always put the club first. Then I met Iris. She's a heap of trouble in a small package and she pinged my radar from the moment I first laid eyes on her. But Iris trusts no one when it comes to her sister. Now I have to make a decision. Changing plans will put the club at risk, but doing nothing will risk them both. I'm not willing to take that risk.

Putting a woman above the club is what got my father in trouble. Now I'm in the same boat. Stupid. Especially since Iris has no idea I've already claimed her.

Chapter One
Iris

"I'll be back for you, Jerrica. You know I will."

"But I don't want you to go!"

I couldn't blame my little sister. I didn't want to go either. Since I'd been emancipated, I couldn't stay. While I knew it was the only way to get my sister out of the group home where we lived, it also meant I had to leave her alone until I proved I could support us both. Since it was so close to my eighteenth birthday, the judge had set that as the day for the evaluation of my living situation. It was reasonable, since the lawyer helping me had said it usually took longer than the three months they were making me wait, but in my opinion it was too damned long. I had to settle for coming to visit her, and I did so every day. If I wasn't working, I stayed all day. If I was, I spent a couple of hours with her afterward. I'd managed to secure an apartment I could afford on one job, but I was working two as long as I could and saving everything I made from it to have something to fall back on in case of an emergency.

"It won't be long. I'll be back tomorrow, honey. You know I would never leave you."

"I do, but..." My sister bit her lip and looked away. I saw the sheen of tears in her eyes and her chin quivering, though. My stomach churned. I knew I was running out of time. I had to get Jerrica out of that horrible place. "It's much harder without you here."

"I know, baby."

"Maybe I should have asked Santa for a better home."

"Santa can't help us, Jerrica. This is all on me. Just hold out a little longer. I'll get you out of here. Just a few more months."

We'd left a huge Christmas Party held by a group of bikers called Black Reign. They were some kind of community benefactors or something. It meant nothing to me other than free food. They held a party for the community's children once a year. If they did anything more the rest of the year, I didn't see it. Still, the celebration had put a smile on Jerrica's face, even if only for a short time. Until I'd had to bring her back to the group home where she lived. Now, without my protection.

Jerrica raised her chin. Even though her eyes were glassy with tears, I could see her determination to do what I'd asked. "OK. I can stand it a little while longer."

I pulled my sister into my arms. "I love you, booboo. It'll all be fine. Just a little while longer."

"I love you too, sissy. Don't forget about me?"

My heart was breaking. Leaving her got harder and harder every day. But I couldn't take her. I didn't have custody of her yet.

"Never! I'll never forget about you!" I gripped her shoulders and looked down into her sweet face. "I've done good. Done what the judge said I had to do. Once I turn eighteen, I'm sure I'll get to bring you home, and we'll be our own little family. March, booboo. We've only got to make it 'til March."

"It'll be like it was before Mom died?"

"Better, even. We won't have to worry about food or if we'll have a safe place to sleep. I'll take care of us."

Jerrica smiled the smile of a trusting child. The smile I'd kill to keep on her face. She was only nine and shouldn't have to worry about shit like this, but the reality was all too different. The group home we'd lived in for three long years was about as far from a home as we could get. Sure, we were fed -- most of the time. But we'd learned the hard way the place wasn't safe. Not all the time. More than one girl had disappeared in the night. I hated leaving Jerrica without my protection, but if I wanted custody of her, I had to start somewhere. Just because I was eighteen wouldn't mean they give her to me. I had to prove I could support us both, and that was exactly what I was doing.

"I'll be back tomorrow. I don't have to work, so I'll be here right after breakfast."

"Will you bring me a peanut butter and jelly sandwich?" Jerrica rarely asked for anything. When she did, this was it.

"Absolutely. I'll bring you two."

"Yeah!" She threw herself into my arms and hugged me tightly. "I love you, sissy."

"Love you too, booboo."

I had a bad feeling. It was an itch between my shoulder blades I couldn't ignore. My instincts were screaming at me to grab Jerrica and run. But that would ruin my chances of getting custody of her. Two-and-a-half more months. I turned eighteen on March fifteenth.

Finally, I let her go, and Jerrica went out of the main hall back to her room. As she was about to round the corner out of sight, she turned and gave me a brilliant smile, waving at me. I waved back, trying to keep from crying. If she saw my distress, she'd come back and refuse to go. It was time for everyone to go to bed. If we created a scene, they might not let me back in. It would definitely hurt my chances of getting custody of her.

I waited until she'd continued on before turning

to go. Once outside, I started the walk home. It was about an hour walk from my tiny apartment to the home, but for once I was glad of it. I needed the time to think. Pacing always helped, and my apartment was too small for much of that.

The next morning when I got there, they wouldn't let me in.

"Jerrica is no longer with us," the administrator told me.

"What do you mean she's no longer with you? I brought her back here last night after the Christmas party!"

"She was adopted. Her new parents left with her about an hour ago."

The man gave me a smile that was more like a sneer. Everything inside me was screaming this was wrong.

"What have you done? Where's my sister!"

"I told you. Now, if you'll excuse me."

He tried to leave, but I stepped in front of him. "You tell me where my sister is. Now!"

"I'm sorry, but, since her parents are deceased and there was no *qualified* relative to take custody of her, the adoption was a closed one. It's a sealed court record."

I felt like my whole world had come crashing down. My little sister. I'd promised her I'd always take care of her, and I'd failed. There was no way she'd been adopted out in the middle of the night. They wouldn't have even been able to process the paperwork that fast. No. She'd disappeared like too many other girls had over the years we'd been there. Logically, I knew this wasn't my fault, but it felt like it. I'd sent her back inside. I'd refused to take her with me. There was no way I could have legally, but it still felt like I should have prevented it.

"If anything's happened to my sister, motherfucker, I'll fucking kill you." I hissed out the words, baring my teeth at him.

"That's it. I'm calling the police." The bastard pulled out his phone, calling 9-1-1.

I waited for the police, knowing this was a battle I couldn't win. The administrator -- Mr. Brown -- had all the right answers, even explaining why the girl had been taken in the dead of night. Saying it had all been arranged beforehand, and they hadn't told either of us because the couple who'd adopted Jerrica hadn't wanted to upset either of us. They also wanted Jerrica to sever all ties with her previous family so she could make a complete and healthy transition to her new family.

Yeah. Fishy as fuck.

When I'd called Mr. Brown out on it all, telling him he was full of shit. I told him -- in front of everyone -- that if my sister was harmed, I'd kill him. I was promptly arrested and escorted off the property. Not my finest moment. Or my most intelligent.

Fortunately, they hadn't done much other than give me a stern talking to and had taken me back to my apartment.

"I know it's hard," one of them said, not unkindly. "But I'm sure your sister will be better off."

"I was supposed to adopt her in less than three months," I said softly. "The judge said if I could prove I could provide for her, I could adopt her when I turned eighteen. All we had in the world was each other."

"Look at it this way. She's got a great new home, and you won't have the responsibility of being a mother at such a young age."

"Jerrica isn't a responsibility," I said hotly. "She's my sister. I love her."

"Do you really?" The cop pinned me with a hard gaze. "If you do, you'll want more for her than this." He gestured at the crappy apartment building where I lived. "Accept it. Move on. And for Christ's sake, don't go around threatening to kill people."

"But other girls have disappeared from there! I'm telling you, there's something not right!"

The cop met my gaze with a level one. "Look. I promise I'll look into them, OK? But you have to face the fact your sister is with another family."

"She'd never have agreed to this." Would she? Maybe everyone was right. Maybe Jerrica would be better off this way.

"Honey, she didn't have a choice. She was a ward of the state. Once they found a suitable home for her, they got another orphan off their books."

"So it's all about money."

"It's about placing children in need with good families." He sighed. "Accept it. Be happy she's got a home with a family who wants and loves her."

"I'm her sister. No one could love her more than me."

"So? Be happy for her. Get on with your life. The faster you accept this and move on, the better you'll feel." He got out of the car and opened the door for me. "I'm sorry, kid. Merry Christmas."

Yeah. Merry fucking Christmas to you too, pal.

There was no way I was letting this go. No one believed me about girls disappearing from the home. The cops didn't believe me about Jerrica being in danger. Why would they? Mr. Brown had a very good explanation. Didn't mean it was true. One thing I knew in my heart was that Jerrica needed me. Even if she wasn't in danger, she needed me.

It was Christmas Day. There wasn't a lawyer's office open, even if I could pay for one. The courts weren't open. There was nothing I could do.

Then I thought about the Christmas party. Maybe there was someone at that place, the Black Reign clubhouse, who could help me. I'd been apathetic toward them when we were there, seeing the party as nothing more than somewhere free I could celebrate Christmas with Jerrica. A place where we could have a hot meal, and she could get presents I couldn't afford to give her. They might laugh in my face. Or run me off and tell me to never come back again. But I had to try. For my sister, I'd try anything.

* * *

Sting

I had no intention of making a trip to Florida for Christmas. I had too Goddamned much to do. Despite Warlock -- the old president of Iron Tzars and my father -- letting his ol' lady manipulate him enough to get the government breathing down our necks, he'd left the club in very good shape. There was no trace of evidence to suggest we'd ever possessed anything from or had any sort of communication with Argent Tech.

The main problem was the division within the ranks. Bev had done a number on several of our members, and I knew there would be some I had to cut. The problem was how to do it. It didn't feel right kicking them out. It wasn't their fault Bev got into their heads. Besides, most of them were younger members or prospects. The older ones knew better. Which was why I found myself rolling into the Black Reign compound on Christmas Day.

"Welcome!" The one they called El Diablo greeted us with a smile and open arms. He was dressed smartly in an expensive-looking suit with diamond-and-gold cufflinks and rings and a lapel pin. He looked like anything other than the president of a motorcycle club. "To what do we owe this great honor?"

I raised an eyebrow. Was this guy for real? I'd known Black Reign was a different sort of MC, but I wasn't expecting this.

"Merry Christmas, El Diablo. I trust your holiday's been good?"

The other man chuckled. "It was very entertaining indeed. Have you come to see Warlock? I'll have someone get him if you have. He's..." He grinned widely. "Otherwise occupied this morning."

"I would have given you a heads-up, but I wasn't sure I was coming till I rolled through the gates." The second I uttered the words, no matter how true, I knew they were a mistake. An MC president didn't just decide to take a road trip to another club. And he certainly didn't roll in on a whim. Especially when the club he rolls into isn't an ally. I stifled my wince. Barely.

Instantly El Diablo's demeanor changed. His features hardened, and I realized why he called himself The Devil. "Not a strong position for the new leader of an MC the likes of Iron Tzars."

"Don't question my abilities." I did my best to mimic my father's deadly tone, knowing I'd shown a weakness to someone who might be an ally, but was certainly no friend. A mistake. One I couldn't afford.

"Don't give me reason to." There was a brief silence while El Diablo and I stared at each other. I imagined he was sizing me up. I knew *I* was sizing *him* up. Underneath that cultured civility was a straight-up killer. I'd dealt with deadly men before. Nature of the beast. But none quite like El Diablo. Even dressed as elegantly as he was, it was easy to believe a killer lurked underneath all his civility. "Now. Tell me the reason for your visit." His mood shifted quicker than shifting sands. The last thing I wanted was to be in too deep with this man or his club, but I wanted my father's advice on this without anyone knowing I was seeking his advice. Since El Diablo had effectively taken away the option of killing Warlock, though I was grateful not to have to kill my own father, I felt like coming here now put me on the wrong side of a debt to this man and his club.

"I need to talk to Warlock."

He smiled. "I figured as much. I sent Rycks to bring him down."

"You said he was otherwise occupied. What does that mean?"

"It means he has a Christmas present of his own he's... unwrapping, shall we say." The slight but clipped British accent was messing with my fucking head. He didn't look or sound like an MC president. Hell, he didn't sound like anything to do with an MC at all.

"Rycks?"

"My right hand."

"The VP?"

El Diablo smiled. "No. He's a trusted friend. One who's been with me a very long time. I rely on him and Archangel to take care of... shall we say, emotional issues that arise in the club." He raised a finger in the air and waved it in a decree. "I'd advise you to have one of your own, Sting. Level heads are very necessary in emotional situations."

"Are you always like this?" I was growing irritated with the other man. I needed to talk to my father. Communicating with him on the phone wasn't something I wanted to do in this matter. I had to have a place to send some of these guys, and he was the only person I trusted to give me an opinion on how to handle this.

He chuckled. "No. I'm usually worse."

"Warlock's on his way." A man came up beside El Diablo. Though I was sure he spoke to the Black Reign president, he looked straight at me. "Told him who his guest was."

"Good! Take him to my office. Warlock and Sting need a quiet place to talk."

"Your office." Though I didn't want to openly show my surprise, it was hard. Why in the world would he open up his office to us? Seemed like a risk on his part, but who was I to argue.

"Yes. Warlock has agreed to be my Enforcer. If I can't trust him, there aren't many here I can trust."

If the man was looking to shatter my control, he did it with that. There was no way to school my expression. I was glad my father had found a place he felt he belonged, but to have him diving back into the inner workings of another club was out of character.

"Does that surprise you, Sting?" El Diablo tilted his head, studying me closely. I hated his attention focused on me. I was making every mistake I could make with this man, letting him see my emotions.

"I think you know it does."

"Well. If it makes you feel better, he fought me on it." The fucker grinned, obviously enjoying this meeting.

"You seem to be enjoying this. Is everyone here for your amusement, or is it just me?" I needed to talk to my dad, but I'd rather meet up on neutral territory if this guy was going to be poking at me the entire time.

"It's not just you, Sting." Warlock entered the room, a woman with him. He held her hand firmly in his. She was little more than a girl, but the way she clung to Warlock left no doubt she was with him. It was one more shock to set my teeth on edge. Also, one more failure in a long line of them on my part in the few minutes I'd been here. El Diablo knew he was getting under my skin, and he thought he knew I disapproved of Warlock's new position within the club and now, also the woman he was with. He'd have been wrong, but I knew it had to look that way. "Come with me."

I probably shouldn't have obeyed him, but it was ingrained in me to do what he said, both as his son and as his vice president in Iron Tzars. I was hopeful El Diablo thought it was respect rather than reflex that had me following my father down the hall to El Diablo's office.

Once inside and with the door closed, Warlock gave me a hard look. He wasn't angry or disapproving. No. This was the look he often got when he was trying to keep his emotions under control.

"It's good to see you, Sting." He lifted his chin, schooling his features.

Yeah. My dad was holding himself back. He probably thought I didn't like his position in this place or the decisions he'd made. Nothing could be further from the truth. I was shocked.

With a sigh, I stepped close to my dad and put my arms around him, clapping him on the back several times. "It's good to see you too, Dad." Warlock hugged me back, holding me tightly for several long seconds. When he pulled back, he blinked rapidly before assuming a blank expression once again.

He cleared his throat, reaching for the woman beside him and putting his arm around her slim shoulders. "Sting, this is my woman. Hope."

"We've met." I held out a hand to the young woman. "Seems things turned out differently than I was afraid they would."

"I know this must be a surprise," she said softly. "It wasn't Warlock's idea." She sounded as if she were trying to defend Warlock. Like she expected me to look down on both of them, but most especially Warlock.

"Might not have been my idea, but it was the best decision I ever had forced on me, sweetheart." He bent to kiss Hope's temple. She blushed and turned into his chest, her arms going around his waist as she shielded her face. Timid little thing.

"Forced on you. Never known anyone to force you to do anything, Warlock. Even Bev couldn't make you do something you didn't want to do." I sneered at my father, wanting to hurt him in the only way I knew I ever could. Not because El Diablo had taken the option away from me. Because I knew, no matter how much me or the rest of the Iron Tzars thought he deserved it, there was no way I could physically hurt my father. "How'd this little thing manage to force you into something? And I'm assuming you mean the fact that she's still here with you and not on her way back to Indiana."

Warlock's gaze snapped to mine. Where before he'd welcomed me, now he looked like he wanted to teach me a lesson I'd never forget. Couldn't blame him. If he'd really taken this girl on as his woman, he should have beaten me to within an inch of my life for the disrespect I'd shown them both.

"Max." Hope patted his chest before rubbing her

face against him. "Let it go. You knew he'd have trouble with this. Can you blame him?"

His hold on her tightened, and he put the other arm around her, kissing the top of her head. "Hope's not Bev, Sting. And it wasn't Hope who forced me into marriage with her. It was my mother."

"Huh." It didn't surprise me. "How'd she accomplish that?"

"She married us without my knowledge. It's all legal. Seems she had no qualms about breaking the law when it suited her." Surprisingly, there was a wistful smile on Warlock's lips. "I'm glad she learned."

I shook my head with a sigh. "So, Hope's my new step-mom."

"She is. And I caution you to really think about your next words, Sting."

I raised my hands, backing up a step. "Nothing to say. It's clear she makes you happy. I can tell by your expression when you look at her."

"Good. Now that's settled. You came to see me. Why?"

That was Warlock. President of Iron Tzars MC. It was comforting to see this side of him again. I was afraid Bev had broken his spirit, especially after he'd had to kill her.

"I need… advice."

He gestured to the couch for me to sit. He sat on the chair and pulled Hope onto his lap. "If you're talking about the club, I'm not sure it's a good idea for you to get advice from me. I fucked things up pretty bad there."

"No, you didn't. It might have looked like you left us open to the CIA, but anything incriminating or leading back to Argent Tech, you were careful to destroy. We actually had a team come in and search the place a few days after you left. They came up empty. Wylde said you'd given him explicit instructions on what to do. He was as thorough as he always is."

"It could as easily have gone the other way, Sting. You know that." His voice was soft as he admitted his own failure. In my book, that made him one of the strongest men I knew.

"Maybe. But I don't think so. If you're guilty of anything, it was loving Bev. She never deserved your devotion."

"No. She didn't. You still haven't told me what you need, Sting."

"There are brothers who are still divided over Bev. You weren't the only one she did a number on."

"Just one more in a long line of failures to the Tzars," he muttered. "What do you need from me?"

"There are six men I need to send somewhere else. Four are prospects, but the other two are fully patched members. None of them are men I want to give up, but they'll never trust each other again. I need to separate them, and I don't want to show favorites by keeping one over the other."

"I can guess which six." Warlock leaned his head back against the chair and closed his eyes for a few seconds before hugging his woman tighter and resting his chin on her head. "Are you going to be on good terms with Cain at Bones?" Bones was an MC in Somerset, Kentucky. Bev's daughter, Chloe, had fled to Bones when Bev had tried to get me to agree to make Chloe my ol' lady. I had no plans to actually take on the girl, but I'd wanted to make sure she was safe. So I'd taken a contingent to Bones only to find Chloe had been claimed by a sniper named Deadeye. She seemed content so I'd left her in his care. Bones was also where

Warlock had snapped Bev's neck. Cain had indicated we should keep an open dialogue, and I tended to agree, but this was a lot to ask another club.

"I'd planned on it. Not sure this is the way to start it out, though."

"Bringing them here creates its own set of problems, but I'll talk to El Diablo. Bones has a sister club in Palm Beach. Tech and Pix would be a perfect fit at Argent. I'll see if there is a way to get them an internship."

"You think Alexi'd be willing to do that? To take them into the Shadow Demons?"

Warlock snorted. "Are you kidding? He's been trying to get those two since the first day he met them. Are they pissed at each other?"

"You could say that. Before I left, I had to put them both on probation. It's a testament to how much they both want to be in Iron Tzars that neither of them just fuckin' quit."

"Good. Giovanni can put them to work. Shadow Demons will be a ton of physical work. Argent will keep their minds occupied. They'll be so busy jumpin' through his hoops they'll forget they're pissed at each other. I can make that transfer happen."

"I'll talk to Cain about the others. See if he's willing to take on a couple of the prospects."

"Good. Sounds like you've got a plan, then."

"Yeah." I scrubbed the back of my neck. "Dad, I'm not cut out for this."

"Sure you are." He sounded so confident I wanted to prove him right. I wasn't sure I could make it happen. "You need to get your feet under you. You're twice the leader I ever was."

That surprised me. "Not sure I'd agree with that assessment."

"You'll be fine, Sting. Just do what you learned over the years. Find your vision for the club and mold it into what you want it to be."

"I want it to be exactly what it's been since I was a kid. An instrument of justice for people in our community who can't get it."

Warlock grinned. "You'll be fine. Believe it or not, your grandmother would be proud of you."

I barked out a laugh. "You're kidding. Right?"

"Nope. Seems she did some soul-searching in her later years. Looking back, if we'd both been better at communication, we'd probably have reached a compromise instead of cutting ourselves off from each other."

I grinned at Hope. "Seems you were good for my gran."

"She was good for me." Hope gave me a small smile.

"Well." I stood, reaching for Warlock's hand. "I should go. I appreciate the face-to-face."

"You're my son. Anything you need, all you have to do is ask."

As I was escorted out by Warlock and Hope, something caught my eye. At the gate was a young girl. She appeared to be arguing with the prospects manning the entry but they weren't giving in to whatever she wanted. She seemed upset, her voice rising the longer the disagreement went on. Hope gasped and pulled away from Warlock.

"Hope!" Warlock lunged for his wife, but Hope managed to dodge him and continue toward the gate.

"Iris?" Hope called out and waved a hand as she hurried toward the girl. "Iris! What's wrong?"

The girl -- Iris -- jerked her head around to find Hope. She was distraught. Angry. "You know my sister! She was with you last night!"

"Yes. Jerrica." Hope looked around. "Is she with you? You're both welcome here if you need a place to stay."

"She's gone!" Tears started streaming from Iris's eyes as she found someone she knew. "Someone took her!"

"Gone? Oh, no! Do you know where?"

Iris shook her head. "Mr. Brown, the administrator at the home, said she was adopted, but I don't believe him. Girls disappear there all the time. Now it's Jerrica!"

"Disappear? What do you mean?"

"There's something going on there, Hope. Since Mr. Brown took over, there have been a bunch of these 'closed adoptions.' He said the new parents don't want a scene and want the children to be able to adjust, to make a clean break from their old lives. But Jerrica would never go along with that."

"Of course, she wouldn't. She loves you." Hope pulled the other woman into her arms. And really, this Iris wasn't more than a girl herself.

"I need help! I need someone to help me find her!"

"Come inside." Hope urged her past the gate and back toward the clubhouse. Warlock shook his head as he acknowledged the prospects.

"I'll take it from here," he said.

I looked at the girl's back and followed Warlock back to the clubhouse, though at a much slower pace. Iris was short and slight. Her clothes were ill-fitting, but clean. Her dark hair was in some kind of tight, elaborate braid atop her head. Though her features were etched in worry and frustration, she was still strikingly lovely. For some reason, I felt compelled to continue to follow her even though this -- whatever it was -- certainly wasn't my fight.

"Just look into it." Iris was pleading with Hope. Hope looked up at Warlock, her eyes wide, all but begging him to help the girl.

"Of course, we'll look into it." El Diablo descended the stairs, a woman on his arm. She was petite and blonde. Maybe close to my age. "Shotgun and Esther will find your sister. If they can't do it themselves, they'll reach out to people who can."

"But if whoever took her figures out you're on to them --"

"They'll do it discreetly. Not to worry, my dear Iris."

She finally let loose a small sob. "I -- I didn't know where else to go. Hope was so nice to Jerrica. Jerrica loves her."

"I love her too, Iris. I'll help in any way I can. Do you need a place to stay?" Hope glanced up at Warlock. "Is it OK if she stays here so she can get information whenever she wants?"

"Of course, it's fine if she stays." This came from the woman with El Diablo. She stepped forward and pulled Iris into her arms in a fierce hug. "We'll take care of everything. I'm Jezebel, El Diablo's wife. We met at the party last night."

Iris nodded. "I remember. Please. She's all I have in the world."

For some reason, this small plea from Iris tore at my heart. I wanted to slay her demons and, more importantly, find her sister and kill whoever had taken her.

"You have us now," El Diablo insisted. "We're all family here."

Iris looked confused but nodded. "If it means

you'll find my sister, then I'm all for it. I don't expect you to do anything for free, though. I don't have much money, but what I have is yours. Maybe I can work around here?"

"Go with Jezebel. She'll take you to Esther, and she and Shotgun can get started. As to payment, making sure you and your sister are safe is the only payment we need."

Iris didn't look like she believed him. Still, she went with Jezebel and Hope.

"You're welcome to stay and help if you wish." El Diablo gave me a welcoming smile. "Maybe bring some of your club down here to go hunting?"

I thought about declining, but then I caught a glimpse of Iris before she disappeared through a doorway. She turned her head and looked straight at me. It wasn't intentional. In fact, her lips parted as her gaze met mine. I thought she inhaled sharply, like the impact of our gazes colliding hit her as hard as it hit me. And it did hit me hard. It felt like a punch to the gut. There was a pull toward her I didn't welcome but couldn't avoid or resist. Which is how I found myself nodding.

"I'll get a team together. I doubt they can be here before late tomorrow evening at best, though. Long ride. Lots to prepare."

"Good!" El Diablo held out his hand. I took it automatically. "I look forward to an alliance with the Iron Tzars. I'm certain it's an arrangement that will be mutually beneficial."

"Look. I have no idea what Warlock told you, but if you're trying to get a line on our tech, don't."

"Argent Tech?" He chuckled. "Boy, Alexi Petrov and I go back further than I care to admit. I guarantee you, I've had access to their services and products far longer than your men have. No. Any relationship our clubs have is purely for alliance building. To make each club stronger in times of need."

I glanced at my father, who shrugged. Under normal circumstances, I'd chalk this up to a bad idea and decline. But, even knowing the devastating consequences if this girl wasn't on the up and up, I was still going to bring the Tzars to Lake Worth to help with this.

"Why do I get the feeling you know more about what's going on with this girl than you're letting on?" I narrowed my gaze at the Black Reign president. He was hiding something.

"Because you're intelligent?" He grinned. "I looked into Iron Tzars long before I invited Warlock into the fold. Your specialty is finding and destroying human trafficking rings."

"I wouldn't call it a specialty. We just happen to have found a few."

"More than a few. Sometimes you can't shut them down completely when you're unable to find the source, but you always free as many as you possibly can and kill those you're able to find who are responsible. I respect that. I also happen to think little Jerrica might have been a victim of one such ring. Shotgun and Wrath have been working to piece together adoption trails on eight girls who vanished from the same group home where Jerrica and Iris lived. So far, they've come up empty. We'd like you to use what you know about how these rings work and help us solve this."

Well. When he put it like that.

"I'll have the men assemble their equipment and roll out. They'll get here ASAP."

"Good. Ask for anything you need. Men,

machines, or money."

"If they can be found, my guys can do it." Hunting was something I was good at. All of the Tzars were. I still had reservations about this being the first major decision I'd made as club president, but the cause was a worthy one, and I knew my dad wouldn't lead me into a situation that was bad for the club. Even if I'd taken his job as president, Warlock was still my dad. "I'll need to see what your men have on this ring."

"I'll have Shotgun hand-deliver it. He can go over it all with you if you like. Fill in any questions you might have."

"I'd appreciate it."

"It's settled, then. Rycks will set you up in a room, and you can start with Shotgun as soon as you're ready."

The rush as I planned for a battle hit me then. Adrenaline was a powerful drug. This was what I lived for. I might question my abilities when it came to being president of an MC like Iron Tzars, but this I was confident in. I'd find Iris's sister. Then I'd figure out what to do with Iris. So help me God.

Chapter Two
Iris

"Do you think they believe me?" I wanted to think they were all taking me seriously, but it was hard when no one else seemed to.

"Honey," Jezebel moved close to me and put a hand on my shoulder. "If they didn't believe you, they'd tell you straight."

"One thing I've learned in the short time I've been here is that these men don't play games. Not like that." Hope was the one person here I might consider trusting enough to believe what she was saying. I was still skeptical, but it was easier to trust her than the others. Mainly because I'd seen how much she loved my sister.

"Can they really do this? Find my sister?"

"Yes." Jezebel answered without hesitation. "If Eden and Shotgun can't readily find her, they have connections who can. They'll find her, and we'll bring her home."

"You seem pretty confident. No one believes me. If it really was a closed adoption --"

"Wrath will find the terms and break it." Jezebel's confidence didn't waver. Her head was up, and there was a satisfied smirk on her face. Like she was eager to see the aftermath of the havoc about to ensue. "He's a lawyer. Currently employed as the district attorney."

"Oh. Well, I guess he can do pretty much what he wants, then."

"Oh, yeah. And if it's not legal, he figures out how to do it anyway. So don't worry. Whether she's been legally adopted or taken by some asshole, we'll get her back. Period."

I sagged into a chair, the weight of my discovery and worry finally taking a toll. Tears threatened, but I swallowed them back. "I'll never be able to repay you guys if you pull this off."

"Yes, you will." Jezebel smiled as she knelt in front of me. "You'll take care of your sister, and you'll be happy. That will be the best repayment we could ever want."

I wasn't sure I believed them, but these people were the first ones to take me seriously. I wasn't ready to give them the benefit of the doubt, but I'd give them any information I could and see what happened.

Another woman entered the room. She had long brown hair reaching down her back in loose curls and kind, brown eyes. She smiled as she entered, greeting the other women warmly.

"Hey, guys!" Her gaze found mine. "You must be Iris. Shotgun's added your sister to the search. We pulled footage from the party to get her picture. We hacked into the city's camera system and are using facial recognition software to find a match. It's a matter of time until we find her." She held out her hand to me. "I'm Shotgun's wife. Eden."

"You've already started?" I took her hand, and she squeezed gently.

"Oh, yeah. We were already working on it. We didn't realize this ring included any of the group homes we hosted for Christmas each year." She frowned. "We thought it was mostly homeless girls and boys. That's bad enough, but to think this ring has someone who's supposed to protect these kids working for them has all the guys here in a snit."

That surprised me. It also gave me real hope that maybe they would find my sister, and this wasn't all lip service. "Why is that? These kids are nothing to you guys."

Jezebel jerked like I'd struck her. "Honey. Those kids are ours as surely as if we'd adopted them. El Diablo and the club pour money into a foundation that is supposed to help each child in those homes go to college or trade school. They can start receiving scholarship money while in high school for classes until they're adopted. It's one of the main reasons we found out something fishy was going on."

"I don't understand. I've never heard about anything like that. Once I was emancipated, I was sent on my way with a smile, a princess wave, and a solid don't-let-the-door-hit-your-ass-on-the-way-out. Was it because I left early?"

"No, honey. You should have had help through high school if you wanted it. In fact, there have been two different group homes we noticed that took money from the foundation, but the recipient in question either never enrolled in school or disappeared altogether." Jezebel had a delicate frown on her face as she spoke.

"In fact," Eden added, "it wasn't until about a week ago we made that discovery. I found where someone had applied for Jerrica to have a tutor for gifted children a couple of months ago. That had to be approved by Wrath, who's in charge of the finances. She got approval a week ago. The first check was cut three days ago. Now, you're telling us she's gone."

"Yes." I felt numb. "Are you telling me this is all an attempt to take money meant for kids in these group homes to have a chance at a better life?"

"Partially." Eden looked very uncomfortable. "We believe it's also an attempt to make it look like these children are still where they're supposed to be. The two homes in question have all applied for scholarships for children taking trade classes or dual-credit college classes. We're trying to track down the children now. So far, all of them have closed adoption records. While the scholarships should end once the adoption process is final, there are exceptions made if there is a financial need in the new home. It rarely happens that a child that age is adopted from a home, so that part of our program hasn't had to be looked at much, but the two homes in question have had about eight of those exceptions applied for in the last six months. Which means, it's not just the home. There is someone in more than one school helping them. Which screams of a trafficking network."

"So, if you take this to the authorities, they'll be able to unseal the adoptions and make sure the children are all safe."

"Perhaps." Jezebel pursed her lips. "But that's not how we operate."

"I don't understand."

"Time is of the essence. If we do this by the law, it may be too late. It will still take time, but we intend to not only find the children, but shut down this shit show permanently."

"Still not getting it." I thought I might, but it seemed a bit extreme for embezzlement.

"You do." Hope's words were soft, and she gripped my hand where she sat on the couch beside me. "We believe this is all part of a human trafficking ring. If we're right, then anyone involved deserves whatever El Diablo dishes out."

I was silent for a moment, letting it all sink in. I knew Jerrica was in trouble, but I think my mind didn't want to go there. It made sense she'd been sold, but the thought of what was happening to her made me want to throw up. Right after I killed someone. Starting with

Mr. Brown.

"I want in on this." I met Jezebel's gaze with a hard one of my own.

She shook her head. "Much as I'd love to tell you the guys would be happy to have the help, they won't. Any of the guys who go into the field on this are all highly trained ex-military. Anyone else stays here. You'll only be in the way. If they are distracted by you, someone could get killed." Jezebel looked sincere. She was as refined as El Diablo seemed to be but had that same core of ruthlessness inside her. The couple was a great match.

"Then I want to know everything they know. I want to be in on any meetings or planning, and I want to hear everything that goes on when they're in the field. I have no idea how you guys operate, but I'm willing to bet there is always someone listening in no matter where the main team is."

Esther ducked her head, but not before I saw the grin on her face. Jezebel cocked her head to the side, studying me. "Yeah. I like you." She nodded her head as if she'd proved a point to herself. "You have spunk. I'll talk to my husband. He has final say."

"It's not a request." I was pushing it, I knew. These women were being nice to me. The club was going to help me find Jerrica. Making demands would get me nowhere, but I couldn't seem to stop myself.

"I definitely like you." To my surprise, Jezebel looked proud of me. "Excuse me. I'll go tell my husband he needs to make a seat at the table for you." It was possible she was making fun of me. I was at least a decade younger than she and vastly less experienced with the male-dominant aspect of a motorcycle club. But I didn't think she was. I thought she might respect me for demanding what I wanted.

Either way, I hoped it would be enough to get me on the inside. Because, once I found out where Jerrica was, there was no holding back. I'd bring my sister home the second I knew where to go, and damn the consequences.

Unfortunately, finding any of the missing children took time. Time they might not have...

* * *

Iris

They'd been at it for more than two months. El Diablo welcomed me into every meeting they had regarding the situation, and it really seemed to be all they were working on. They were careful how they worded it so none of them sounded like they were glad Jerrica had been taken, but it seemed like Jerrica going missing was the break they needed. Unlike the other children, they had a close timeframe for when Jerrica had been taken, and the trail was fresh. Didn't mean it was easy going.

Also, one of the men working on finding Jerrica... intrigued me. I didn't want to notice him. Didn't want to think about him instead of my sister, but Sting was fascinating to me. He wasn't as old as the others and seemed unsure of himself at times. Other times, he took charge from men far older and seasoned than he was. I tried not to stare at him, but he was in charge. I justified my preoccupation with him because he had the final decision in anything that happened. The reality was far less noble. I pulled my attention back to Shotgun, needing to keep my eyes on what was important.

"There's so many roadblocks and hairpin turns, me and Esther are having trouble breaking through." Unlike most of the time I'd seen Shotgun, he was agitated and frustrated as hell today. "These fuckers better hope someone other than me finds them, 'cause if I get to deal with them, I'mma throw a motherfucker a beatin' he'll never fuckin' forget." The normally easygoing man was ready to go to war. Anyone could see that.

"Have you reached out to Giovanni Romano?" Unlike Shotgun, El Diablo was calm as ever.

"Last night. After I realized we were getting nowhere. He said he'd get Bones involved in this too. And Ripper at Salvation's Bane."

"Good. With all of us working on this, it's only a matter of time. Questions?" When no one voiced any, he dismissed everyone.

I followed Shotgun out of the room. He was muttering to himself and seemed none too happy. It was a bad time to bother the man, but I wanted to watch over his shoulder. All the information was coming to him, and I wanted to be there when he got the word Jerrica had been found.

He went to his and Esther's office, and I was hot on his heels. He did a double take when he went to shut the door and I slipped in before he got it shut.

"Oh, shit! You OK?"

"Yeah. You didn't get me with the door." I grinned, trying to lighten the mood. "You don't mind if I hang out here, do you? I promise I won't say a word or get in the way."

Shotgun scrubbed a hand over his face, like he was bone tired. Esther looked up from her computer and smiled at me. "Of course, you can stay. Don't mind him. He's cranky if he doesn't get a solid eight hours."

"Am not cranky." Shotgun put his chin up stubbornly.

Esther rolled her eyes. "He's totally cranky."

He sighed, deflating. "Yeah. I'm cranky."

"I know this is stressful, and you guys didn't have to take this on, but I want you to know I appreciate it. I can't find my sister without your help."

"Oh, Iris!" Esther got up and came to me, hugging me fiercely. "You never have to thank us for that. Yes, it's stressful, but it's stressful because none of us want any of those children in danger one second longer than they need to be."

"The longer it takes me to find them, the more likely it is they'll be hurt." Shotgun sounded like he was only half listening to the conversation. He was scrolling through images and camera feeds on four different monitors. It didn't seem like he blinked as he worked.

"Just give us some time to work through this." Esther gave me an encouraging smile. "We'll find her and everyone else."

I sat in a chair behind the pair and watched them work. They spoke softly to each other, Shotgun working through his task while Esther studied one electronic document after another. I squinted and leaned forward and realized she was going through adoption records.

"How did you get access to those?" I couldn't prevent the question from popping out. Esther looked back over her shoulder and grinned. "Important people in high places. Wrath sent these to me. It's time consuming, but we're being careful not to leave a digital footprint."

"So nothing comes back to you when you find these assholes."

"Now you're getting it."

Shotgun snorted. "I remember a day when you'd have balked at that, doll." He reached over and squeezed his wife's hand.

"True. But I've realized over the years I've been here that sometimes bad things need to happen to bad people." The smile she gave her husband was intimate and lovely. For the first time in my life, I realized what I'd been missing. Adult affection. I didn't mean sex. But the closeness only two people who loved each other had. I was barely an adult, and only because I got a judge to say I was, but I'd lived my life like an adult since our mother died -- taking as much responsibility as I could for myself and Jerrica. I wanted a man to look at me like Shotgun looked at Esther and to stand between me and the rest of the world when I needed him to.

I sat back, remaining quiet. All day. I didn't leave unless they left, and that was only to go to the bathroom. Someone brought them food and made sure there was plenty of coffee and soda.

We were there three days before the first break came. After that, things started moving quickly. Up to a point. It had been exactly eighty-nine days since my sister had been taken. To say I was giving in to despair was a severe understatement.

"There are kids in a warehouse on the outskirts of town next to the docks." Shotgun gave a clipped account, sounding as angry and agitated as the last time the whole group had major information to share. "I've counted six kids, but there could be more. And they're getting ready to move them. Like in the next couple of hours." He ran his hands through his hair. Esther placed a hand on his arm and rubbed his back, like she was soothing a wounded animal. "I doubt there is any way to move in before they're gone without risking one or all of them getting killed. We simply don't have time to get Sting's team all the information they need to plan the operation."

There was a long silence before El Diablo spoke. "Do you know what their patterns are? Will they immediately pick up a new group of children?"

"Oh, yes." Esther stepped up this time. "We know their patterns. We've gone back over camera feeds everywhere a camera is pointed even remotely toward that warehouse. Most were disabled or destroyed over the past six or eight months, but I found some two blocks over that happened to be pointed at a decent angle. It wasn't perfect, but, with the help of Giovanni and some really nifty image-enhancing software, as well as the citywide access he got us, we were able to piece together their movements over the last six months. So we moved it back another six to establish patterns. That went far faster because it took them a while to disable the security without anyone making too big a fuss. They offload the children and pick up new ones on their way back to the warehouse. Exactly ninety days later, they do it all again."

"Same time?"

"Every time."

"So, if they get this group off before we're ready to confront them, there will be another group within... what? Hours?"

"Yes." Shotgun crossed his arms over his chest. "I don't like this, El Diablo. We're not going to be ready to be able to help this group, which likely has Jerrica in it."

"Does Giovanni know the full situation?" El Diablo was all business, his accent clipped and his deep voice commanding the room.

"He does. He's sweating as much as we are, though he won't admit it. Pulled Merrily in to help him from what Alexi said." Shotgun shook his head. "Even he doesn't think we have time to pull this off. But he's got the whole fuckin' city hacked. He'll know where they go and who they're with. We'll get them all back. Just not today."

"You have to!" I couldn't stay silent any longer. "Jerrica's already been through enough! All of them have! It's been three months! They've probably already hurt the kids they took. You can't let these people... *sell* my sister!"

"I know you're upset." El Diablo stood and crossed the room toward me. He wasn't at all threatening about it, but I still backed up a step. Right into Sting.

He wasn't from Black Reign, but he was the man tasked with getting my sister. I gasped and turned to face him, knowing I was trapped between him and El Diablo. For some stupid reason, my hands landed squarely on his T-shirt-covered chest. Muscles rippled beneath my touch, and I gasped at the unexpected pleasure those sensations caused. Sting just looked down at me, tilting his head and narrowing his gaze, studying me like he might an insect. Right before he squashed it.

I tried to snatch my hands away from him, but Sting stepped back into my space, trapping my hands against him. "You let me worry about getting your sister back. It's what my club does." His thumb feathered back and forth over my hand before he glanced down at where we touched.

My fantasies about Sting hadn't decreased despite my pep talk to myself. If anything, I craved his attention even more. What woman wouldn't? He was dangerous. Anyone could tell by looking at him. There wasn't anything he missed, and he kept a tight rein on his club.

There were several men who'd come in a day after I arrived here so distraught and looking for help. Though Sting's men spoke with various members of Black Reign occasionally, they mostly kept to themselves. Sting had them going over blueprints and maps all day, every day as they discussed the layout of the city and its various problems. And they trained. Hard. I noticed several of the girls in the club approached the newcomers, but none of the men seemed to care. They kept about their business and never mixed business with pleasure. All of them were big, powerful men. But Sting was the one who caught my eye. This was the first time he'd ever so much as looked my way.

Sting dropped his hands, and I snatched my own away as he addressed El Diablo. "I'll get all the info from Shadow Demons and be ready before they bring the next bunch of kids to the warehouse. We'll get rid of whoever is still there. When they show up with the new group of children, we'll take them out. By that time, Giovanni should have everything we need to rescue the group they're getting ready to offload." He sounded so calm. So sure of himself. I wanted to believe, but this was Jerrica. If there was any way to prevent her from being sold in the first place, I was going to figure it out. By myself if I had to.

"I promise you, Iris," El Diablo assured. "We'll get your sister back as quickly as possible."

I said nothing, afraid I'd sound ungrateful or irritated. Years of living in a group home had taught me when to keep my mouth shut. This was one of those times.

The discussion continued, but I was done listening. I knew where Jerrica was being held. I knew it was guarded. I knew they were getting ready to move her. I might not be able to take out the men in the warehouse, but I could rescue Jerrica. If I could get anyone else out, I would, but Jerrica would be my first priority. With that thought in mind, I slipped out of the meeting and out of the clubhouse. I'd make a plan on the way.

Chapter Three
Sting

That girl. That fucking girl.
Iris.
I got it now. I understood how my dad could give up his club for a woman. And the woman he'd allowed to betray us wasn't even the woman he ended up with. If what he felt for Bev had been even half of what I just experienced with Iris, I could understand everything he'd done. Which meant that he wouldn't just kill anyone who threatened his wife, Hope. He'd *annihilate* them. I knew this because the second Iris's hands landed on my chest, whoever had taken her sister wasn't going to die the quick, painless death we usually brought to human traffickers. Oh, no. They were going to die hard and slow. Over days. Weeks. Why? Because they'd hurt Jerrica and, by extension, Iris. No one would ever hurt that girl again as long as I lived and breathed. It didn't matter if drawing it out risked getting caught. I would get justice for this woman. No matter the cost.

I looked around the room until I found Warlock. He was looking at me intently. I glanced at Iris before meeting Warlock's gaze squarely and holding it while the conversation around us continued. The other man merely raised an eyebrow before lifting his chin, an indication he understood Iris was mine.

She stepped back, ducking her head. Not surprising given she was squarely in a meeting where men easily two or three times her size were discussing how best to kill a bunch of motherfuckers. I wasn't ready to take her in hand at the moment, so I focused on the rest of the meeting.

"I wonder why they pick up new kids on their

way back from selling the last bunch." Shotgun continued to peck on his laptop. Even when he wasn't in his office, he was still working, picking up feeds from the Shadow Demons. Shadow Demons was a club in Rockwell, Illinois. They weren't exactly MC, but they operated much the same. They liked to think of themselves as one-percenters who just happened to be billionaires. Alexi Petrov was their president and co-CEO of Argent Tech along with Azriel Ivanovich and Giovanni Romano. They were the bridge between our clubs. I had the feeling El Diablo would one day be the muscle for all of us, and I wasn't sure how that sat with me.

"To keep exposure to a minimum. They only leave that warehouse with kids in tow once every ninety days." The guy who spoke -- Wrath -- looked more like a corporate lawyer than a biker. Not surprising since he was the District Attorney for this area. From what I understood, he'd been shoved into that role several years before with the intention of finishing out the four-year term his predecessor had started before leaving the position under mysterious circumstances. Wrath had done such a good job of cleaning up the corruption that the people had elected him for a second and then a third. I couldn't deny someone that high up in the city and district was a wonderful pet to have. "It's a smart move. Only mistake they've made is making the moves so predictable."

"Oh?" El Diablo raised an eyebrow. "Do continue."

Wrath shrugged. "They leave at the same time every ninety days. Exactly. On the nose. They take the same route, though they do use different vehicles. Same driver. Same muscle. Same drop-off location. The men who take possession of the children are just as predictable, only not as polished. There is one fifteen-second call made exactly seventy-two hours before they move the kids. Giovanni listened in on the last one. We'll know once we see them leave, but it sounded like they confirmed the move was still happening and gave the number of kids to be moved."

El Diablo steepled his fingers in front of him. "Seventy-two hours. Every time."

"Giovanni found the phone records. And it wasn't easy. Other than their predictability, they're pretty careful and very hard to trace." Wrath delivered the information with a casual air. Like he didn't really give a fuck. His eyes told a different story. He wanted these fuckers. Badly.

"Exactly. To the hour. Initiated by the warehouse team."

"OCD?"

"Don't know. Don't care. But it means we have a reliable timeline to work with."

"I'd prefer to have at least one more test on that phone call, but we can't risk the kids." Samson, the vice president of Black Reign, sat back in his chair in the corner of the room. He was usually quiet, staying in the background. "The second crew doesn't appear to be as conscious of time constraints as the warehouse group. Like they don't understand they need to get in and out quickly. Making the first party wait increases the likelihood of all of them getting caught."

"Precisely." Wrath wrapped his knuckles on the table. "And that's how we'll find them."

"Has it ever happened?"

"Not that we can find."

"Good," I said, needing to assert myself in all this ego. While I thought I might respect this club and her members, they'd asked Iron Tzars to do this. El Diablo had asked *me* to bring my men down here to work this. We hadn't volunteered for it. "I want Wylde in the middle of this. He's my intel guy, and he and Brick will put our operation together from here forward. He should have been in there with Shotgun and Esther more the last two months instead of with the rest of the club. Any help you want to lend will be appreciated, but I need you to understand that if we're doing this, we do it my way, and I'm taking over from here."

El Diablo grinned. "Of course, Sting. You have complete control over every aspect of these operations. Ask for anything you need." He glanced around the room at his men. "We are completely at your service. We'll do as much or as little as you require."

"As long as we understand each other."

"Well," El Diablo stood, prompting everyone else to do the same, "I suggest we all get to work. Wrath, Shotgun, give Sting as much information as you can come up with. Samson, see to it the men from Iron Tzars have whatever they need." His gaze shifted back to me. "There's no way to rescue the children at the warehouse tonight. Is that correct?"

"Not safely. If we try to do this at the warehouse tonight, there is a significant risk of collateral damage. I will not risk hurting -- or killing -- the very children we're trying to rescue."

The other man nodded crisply. "Agreed. So, we have three months to get ready?"

"No. We concentrate on the rescue of this group *after* they leave the warehouse. We know their patterns. We know where they're going. So we scout out their destination and watch. If there is a safe way to rescue all of the children later tonight, we take it. If not, we'll continue to follow them until we find our opening."

"That's the unpredictable group. We have an idea of what they'll do. Even though they seem to follow the same patterns, they're not as exact." Wrath furrowed his brow, concentrating solely on me. I could all but see the wheels in his mind turning, running through all the options.

"And the warehouse?" Samson's gravelly voice cut through the room unexpectedly.

"It's not going anywhere. As long as we're not seen, as long as anything we do tonight doesn't have blowback, the men at the warehouse won't know there was a problem until the designated contact time one week before the exchange. Eighty-seven days from today. That's an eternity to plan. But we won't need that long. We'll need long enough to make sure anyone inside is part of their operation. After that? The whole crew dies. If you want us to follow the trail further, you'll have to extend more resources and equipment to us."

"We'll discuss that once we have little Jerrica back." El Diablo sat back, a look of supreme satisfaction on his face. "Good." He gave me a crisp nod, looking supremely satisfied. "Very good."

"I'll get my crew into position."

"Keep in touch at all times, Sting." Samson stood and indicated the door. "I'll walk you out and inspect your gear with you."

I looked around the room and noticed Iris wasn't there. I'd opened my mouth to say something when Jezebel opened the door. Her gaze landed on her husband, her expression tight.

"Iris is gone."

"What?" I barked out the question before I could censor myself.

Jezebel addressed El Diablo, not even looking at

me. "She hopped in an Uber and left."

"Did she even have money? Why did you let her leave?" I had no idea why I was losing my shit. Add it to the long list of fuck ups I'd made. I needed to be rational and was failing miserably.

"Watch your tone with my wife, Sting. I like you. Doesn't mean I won't kill you."

I took a breath. He was right. I needed to get myself together, but a panic seized me that I couldn't stem. I knew in my heart where she was headed. "That fuckin' warehouse," I muttered. "She's headed to that fuckin' warehouse."

Which meant there was going to be a massive change of plans. And I was going to need every single member of my club present to pull this off. I pulled out my phone and sent a group text.

All hands on deck. Bike garage.

Less than five minutes later, the nine members of Iron Tzars I'd brought with me gathered near our equipment, scouring over the maps of the area.

"What the shit, Sting? Big fuckin' change of plan, don't you think?" Wylde scrubbed a hand over the back of his neck. "I'll do whatever you say, but this seems a bit extreme."

"Prez knows what he's doin'." Brick, my vice president, spoke quietly as he studied the map of the area around the warehouse and where we expected the kids to be taken. The man didn't look up or speak loudly, but Wylde didn't say another word.

"Team one will be on the kids. You stick to them like fuckin' glue." I gave the order to Brick. He was an ex-con. Did twenty-five years in prison.

When I met him, he'd struggled to fit into society but had thrived in the Tzars. Of all the men I knew, I trusted Brick the most to complete any task I set him on. He'd never failed me and had been at my side when things had gone wrong more than once. Not only did he help me clean up any messes, but he'd taken the heat instead of letting it fall to me. More than once I was afraid he'd end up back in jail, but me or Warlock had always managed to keep him out. We'd fought over it once. I'd busted his balls for taking the heat on what could have ended up with him facing another murder conviction. He'd told me then he didn't care what it cost him. He'd always have my back. I'd met him when I was twenty-three and he was forty-five. Six years ago. It was like the age gap between us made little difference. He was my right hand. True to his word, he'd always had my back. Which was good, because I was depending on him more than I ever had.

"We won't lose them. Who do you want to go with me?"

"You choose your team. You will not engage them unless you feel there is a danger you're gonna lose them. Under no circumstances are you to lose Jerrica."

"I won't lose any of 'em, Prez." Brick addressed me as Prez as a show of respect, but also to remind some of the older guys in no uncertain terms that I was in charge now. Not Warlock. "Gimmie Cyrus, Roman, and Morgue. The four of us can handle it."

"Good. Atlas, Shooter, and Snake are with me. Wylde, you set up with Shotgun and keep an eye on things from here. I want you watchin' every fuckin' thing. If there's a fuckin' rat in that warehouse, I wanna know about it. Same with the kids. Use every resource you can to have eyes on them from the time they exit that warehouse until they are safely back here." I looked around the circle of men who were Iron Tzars. "No mistakes. Get the kids to safety. Kill every other motherfucker in the area. Use your best discretion."

Brick gave me a crisp nod, then left with his men to plan their part in this venture. There was every possibility Iris would either be captured or killed before we got there, but I wasn't writing her off yet. I wasn't going to storm Hell with a water pistol either. If we took out the warehouse and the people in it tonight, we wouldn't be going in blind. I'd know exactly who was inside.

Atlas crossed his arms over his chest. As the club's Sergeant at Arms, he was going to want answers. So I leveled my gaze on him. "She's mine, Atlas."

"Does she know that?" Atlas grinned, obviously amused at my expense. "'Cause I kinda think she hasn't gotten the memo."

"She will."

He shrugged. "Have you even said more than two words to her?"

"Not your business." Motherfucker was enjoying this way too fucking much. Can't say I didn't deserve it. "Don't matter much anyway. Girl could be in trouble. We can't abandon her."

"Is it abandonment if she ran off straight into trouble?" The way Snake frowned told me he didn't like the situation. He'd been in the club for more than twenty years and had been one of a few who'd voted against me becoming president. Couldn't say I blamed him. The man had watched me grow up. Several of them had. He had come around somewhat but kept a close eye on me.

"Sometimes it feels like I'm a kid riding a bike when the adults refuse to take off the training wheels." I muttered the resentment under my breath before addressing Snake. "You don't want to be part of this, you should have said so from the beginning. Brick could have left your ass back in Evansville. You want out? Tell me now. I ain't plannin' somethin' only to have a member of my fuckin' team balk at the last fuckin' minute."

Snake raised his hands in surrender. "You're the prez. I'm just not sure changing the plan for one girl is a good idea. Not when we don't have long to plan for it."

"Ain't a democracy, Snake." I turned my attention to Atlas and jerked my head in Snake's direction. "Find me someone in this club you trust to make up the third man in Brick's team. And get this fuckin' pussy outa my sight."

"Hey, Sting. Just relax." Snake chuckled like it was all a big fucking joke. "No need to get out of sorts. I'm just tryin' to inject some reason into the team. You've got something other than the job on your mind."

"You think I'm makin' the same mistake my old man made?"

"Didn't say that."

"Didn't have to." I gave Snake my hardest stare.

Atlas put a hand on his shoulder, and Snake shrugged him off. "You can't run off everyone who questions you, son. We only do it for your own good. And for the good of the club."

"I'm the fuckin' president, Snake. I can do what the fuck I want. There's a chain of command. You don't like something, you take it to Brick or Atlas. If they think it's worthy of my attention, they will bring it to me. Now. Get the fuck out. You're confined to quarters until we're ready to leave for home, or until I need you."

"Goddamned stubborn pup." Snake stalked off, getting in a parting shot.

Atlas shot off a quick text. I had no idea who he texted, but I suspected Warlock. As Enforcer of Black Reign, he'd be responsible for anyone with discipline problems.

"You can't always call in my father for back up, Atlas."

"Nope. And I didn't this time. I texted Black Reign's enforcer. The last thing we need is for that son of a bitch causing trouble in another club's territory." I met Atlas's gaze. "You know you're gonna have to dismiss him from Tzars."

"Not unless it's absolutely necessary. I'm not ready for what that entails."

Atlas nodded. "At least you can admit it. Brick can take care of him. He would anyway."

"No. Anyone leaves the club for any reason, it's my responsibility. So, if I have to kick him out, I won't do it when I'm angry at him. I'll do it with a clear head and after I've discussed it with you and Brick. Not before."

Atlas inclined his head, a slow smile forming on his lips. "Yeah. You're gonna do fine." His grin widened. "Pup." I swung my fist at Atlas, but he easily ducked it, chuckling the whole time.

"We're heading out." Brick approached, a hard expression on his face. "Anything I need to take care of?"

I shook my head. "Not now. We'll worry about it later. For now, your job is the kids."

"Understood, sir." With a nod to me and a quick glance at Atlas, Brick stomped back to his team. Brick would be there when they moved the children. He would do as I'd instructed, and he'd be efficient about it. Which was a good thing, because I was going to have my hands full with the warehouse.

"We've only got until dark, Prez." Atlas clapped a hand on my shoulder. "I'll see if El Diablo can spare Jekyll."

"He'll be a good fit?"

"He will. More importantly, he's a lot like Brick. Loyal to a fault. He and I grew up together. Reconnected when we rolled in here. Went through a lot when we were kids."

"Good. He gonna have a problem takin' orders from me?"

Atlas shrugged his massive shoulders. The man was aptly named. "Can't speak to that. But I wouldn't consider him if I thought he'd be a problem."

"Jekyll it is, then. I want to be in place by full dark. Shotgun and Esther said the men from the warehouse should be back with a fresh group of kids an hour after that."

"Sounds like a plan. I'll fill Jekyll in on everything and meet you here in three hours."

"Sure he'll join us, are you?"

"Yep." With a grin, Atlas turned to leave.

I looked at the compound gate. Everything in me demanded I follow Iris. I barely knew the woman, and only from afar. I knew nothing about her other than she was super protective of her sister and had more determination than was good for her. "Damned woman should have trusted me to take care of this."

"Well, she doesn't know you."

Warlock came up behind me. I turned to look over my shoulder at him and scowled. "So? She knew El Diablo asked me to do this. She knows him and this club well enough to come here when she needed help. She should have trusted them."

"You're gonna have a hell of a time, Sting. This is going to be amusing."

"You can be a real dick sometimes, Dad."

"Just sometimes?"

I wanted to smack the grin off his face. I had certainly fallen hard for a woman I didn't know. The only person who could read me better than Brick was Warlock. "Watch it, old man."

He sobered then. "Heard you had words with Snake."

"I did. He's gonna give me grief."

"Always did me. Want my advice?" I raised an eyebrow, knowing Warlock would give me his advice whether I wanted it or not. "Cut him loose. I shoulda done it years ago, but I was too busy letting Bev ruin my life."

"You think he'll continue to cause trouble, then?"

"I know he will. He has for years. Had his sights set on being president since before I was voted in years ago. He will question everything you do and sow seeds of discord everywhere. Especially with the older men. You've got Brick and Atlas firmly in your corner, so they can keep it under control, but that's one more nail in your coffin." His expression was hard. "The best way to keep those guy's respect is to do what you have to do as quickly as you can. In fact, take care of it before you leave to go back to Indiana. Use this job as leverage to get Black Reign to clean up the mess."

"Is that what you'd do?" I knew what his answer would be, but I needed to ask the question.

"Without hesitation. Don't make the same mistake I did. You want Iris? Great. Take her. Make her yours. But keep your eyes on the club and her members."

"Understood."

I headed up to my room. I needed a power nap so I was fresh when this went down. The last three months had been filled with sleepless nights and planning. My head hurt sometimes with all the things rolling around up there. This was a mission I could not fuck up.

When I reached my room, I locked the door and shot off a text to Atlas telling him where I was. Then I stretched out on the couch and shut my eyes. I was as prepared as I could be. It was time to trust my team and be as rested as I could be for the coming battle.

Chapter Four
Iris

I sat outside a warehouse on the edge of the industrial shore area. Ships on- and off-loaded their cargoes about a quarter mile away. The warehouses were easily accessible to the road and any truck ferrying cargo. This warehouse was on the remote edge. Close enough to be part of the complex, but far enough away not to draw attention. No one had come or gone, but it wasn't fully dark yet. I figured anything they did would be under the cover of darkness.

This was a stupid idea. There was no way I stood a chance of actually rescuing Jerrica. Not only was I not strong enough to actually win a fight, I was absolute shit at fighting. The only thing I could hope for was to be captured and be put with Jerrica and any other kids inside. At least then I could provide a small layer of protection for her.

As if I'd summoned them, the door opened, and two men stepped outside the warehouse. One was on his phone, the other scanning the area like he knew what he was looking out for. Yeah. I didn't have a chance in hell of taking Jerrica from these men if they had her.

I was about to back my way out of the area and try to find a better way in when a hand clamped over my mouth and pulled me down to the pavement. I tried to fight off my attacker, but he was infinitely stronger than me, trapping me face down between the hard ground and his equally hard body. My heart raced as I tried to buck him off me, but he was so Goddamned heavy! He didn't seem to feel anything even though my feet connected with his shins more than once.

"Knock it off, Iris. It's me."

That voice…

I stilled. When I did, he slowly removed his hand from my mouth.

"Sting?" We hadn't spoken to each other aside from in meetings, and I'd never addressed him directly. He always seemed to be watching me, though. It was as unnerving as it was exhilarating. Sting was the type of man you didn't defy. He was hard and unbending. Anyone could see by the way he handled his club his word was law. Now he had me under his control. The thought should have been disconcerting. Instead, I felt an overwhelming sense of relief.

"The one and only, little hellcat." His deep, rumbly growl at my ear made my insides shiver. God, this man was potent! The heat from his body was scorching. Even more so with his breath in my ear. In another situation I'd be swooning. Now I was pissed off.

"What are you doing here?" I hissed my question.

"Could ask you the same thing."

"I'm trying to rescue my sister since you're too big a pussy!" Lashing out at him wasn't the smartest thing I'd ever done, but he'd scared the life out of me.

"Always intended to go after your sister, Iris." He didn't sound angry or annoyed. Just matter-of-fact.

"You said it was too big a risk! That you didn't have time to set things up or whatever!"

"Honey, your sister's already been moved. Brick's got a crew following her. They will get her to safety when they see an opening, and she'll be safe and sound back with you in less than twenty-four hours."

"What?" Panic seized me. "They've… they've already moved her? Oh, no!" I struggled anew, doing everything I could to get the big bastard off me. Still, he didn't budge.

"Take it easy, little hellcat. We've got this under control. All you have to do is stay where I put you while we take care of these bastards. They're bringing in a new group of kids. When they get here, we'll rescue the kids and erase the bad guys. Yeah?"

"But you said it was too risky!"

"I said we'd never get her if we tried to take her at the warehouse because we only had an hour to plan and get set up. Not nearly enough time to do it without risking Jerrica. I never said we'd leave her."

I stilled beneath him, looking back over my shoulder. "You promise?"

"I do, hellcat. I ain't no saint, but I'd never leave a little girl in the hands of monsters because I was afraid to go in and take her. Only wanted to minimize the danger to her as much as possible. But we got eyes on her. Brick thinks the risk is acceptable, or it becomes more dangerous to her for them to wait any longer, he'll strike and risk everything to bring her back safe."

"You really believe that." It wasn't a question. I could see it in his eyes.

"I do. Now. 'Cause you jumped the gun and didn't trust us, I gotta take care of these fuckers a little quicker than I'd like. I'll be spankin' your ass later for not trustin' me on this."

Two thoughts went through my head. First was, "Yes, sir. May I have another?" I wasn't about to say that out loud. So I settled with something a little more outraged.

"Touch me, and I'll find a way to kill you."

Sting chuckled. "Yeah? We'll see. In the meantime, I need you to stay here. Let me and my boys do what we're trained to do. I'll come back for you, and we'll meet up with Brick so you can be with your sister."

I sucked in a breath. Tears threatened. I wanted to believe him. So bad! Looking up into his eyes, I thought I might. Sting lifted his weight off me slightly, and I rolled to my back. To my surprise, he settled himself back on top of me. I should have felt trapped. Instead, I kept seeing us like this in a different setting. A soft mattress beneath me while Sting's hard body was above me.

Without thinking too much about it, I lifted my hand to his face, stroking his short beard. He let me, even grinning down at me. Then he lowered his face to mine and kissed my lips in a soft, lingering caress.

I could have sworn the sky lit up with fireworks. I know I whimpered as I opened my mouth in a soft gasp. Sting grunted, sweeping his tongue inside my mouth in a slow, gentle glide. He only did it once before ending the kiss and lifting himself to look down at me.

"I'll finish that once we're in my own territory, hellcat." He grinned, his gruff voice sending a thrill through me.

I blinked up at him. This was a really bad idea. He was managing me, and I was letting him. When his grin turned into a smirk, I found my backbone and determination. I shoved him off me. Rather, I shoved, and he got to his feet, then reached for me. Rather than waiting for me to take his hand -- which I would never! -- he grabbed my arms and hauled me to my feet.

"Come on. You can wait in the truck. Everything goes without a hitch, you'll ride with me. Anything goes sideways, you'll be in a safe place, and Atlas'll get you back to the compound."

"You can't just dump me off like a naughty

child!"

"Well, you shouldn't have acted like one." His grin was positively panty-melting, but I wasn't letting it get to me. This man was entirely too cocky for my liking.

"Are you sure my sister isn't in there?"

"Absolutely, hellcat. Brick's got his team on her with instructions to get all of them to safety. If they can't get everyone, they will get Jerrica or die trying."

He sounded so confident. And the expression on his face was almost playful when I knew he was anything but. I'd seen this man for weeks. Every day. We hadn't interacted much, but he rarely smiled and never joked. This was a whole other side of him I'd had no idea existed. He seemed less intimidating, but I knew better.

I didn't really want to do what he said -- because he'd taken for granted I'd follow his orders -- but I found myself letting him take my hand and lead me to the big Bronco waiting two blocks away. He opened the door to the back passenger's side and guided me inside.

"Wait here. I'll be back as soon as I can and take you to your sister."

This was insane. I didn't know this guy. Good kisser aside, I wasn't sure I even liked him. He was so abrasive in the club atmosphere that this other side of him was throwing me. Maybe all he wanted to do was manage me. Maybe after they got the children out of the warehouse, he'd go back to ignoring me. My stomach rebelled at the thought, rolling in grief I had no business feeling. When we were at the clubhouse, every time his gaze met mine it was like a physical caress. It was like he could see into my soul. There was such wicked promise in those unspoken exchanges I already thought of him as mine. Which was stupid. Men like him didn't want a little innocent like me. It was for the best, really. Once this was done and I had Jerrica back, she needed to be my focus. Not a man who was completely unattainable and would only break my heart.

But that kiss...

Admittedly, that was my first kiss. Living in a group home with a bunch of girls wasn't exactly a place to meet guys. At least, not of the non-creepy variety. There were always the couples coming to visit and see if there were children they were interested in. The only ones interested in me and Jerrica were men and sometimes women who had plans in mind for one or both of us that weren't limited to providing a nurturing home environment.

I'd never been interested in the boys at school, the little we got to interact with them, but older guys weren't for me either. I'd noticed most of the women at Black Reign had men who were much older than they were. I didn't think I could do that. Sting, however, while older than me, didn't give me that icky feeling most older men did. Thinking back to when he'd had me on the pavement before, I hadn't felt threatened. Even before I knew who had me, when I'd fought to get him off me, I hadn't felt that bone-deep panic I should have.

I was so lost in thought I jumped and gave a little squeal when the door to the Bronco opened, and three girls scrambled in. The dome lights didn't engage, so it was dark inside. I couldn't see their faces, but as they pressed against me, I could feel them tremble.

"Come with me, Iris." Sting's deep, gruff voice was commanding, and I started moving before I really thought about it.

"Iris?" One of the girls squealed out my name. I squinted, trying to see, but it was impossible.

"Who is it?"

"It's us, Iris." Another of them answered. "Daisy, Monica, and Clover."

I gasped. "What?" I reached for the girls, pulling Daisy and Monica close while little Clover crawled into my lap. Clover was only six, while the other girls were twelve. They were wrapped in thick blankets, but otherwise, didn't seem to have any clothes on.

"They took us," Daisy said bitterly. "Fuckers tried to..." She trailed off and shuddered against me.

"Why are you with these guys?" Monica spoke softly, almost a whisper. "Aren't they just as bad as the others?"

Clover hadn't said a word, but her arms were wound tightly around my neck, and she shivered continually. I thought she was weeping silently, and that was like a dagger to my heart. It wasn't surprising. The girl hadn't spoken since she'd first come to the home a year before. I suspected this incident wouldn't help her along any.

"They aren't like the ones who took you, Monica. They're here to help, and to make sure this doesn't happen to anyone else."

"I'm not going back to that fucking place." It was no surprise Daisy felt that way. I'm sure they all did. I sure as hell did. There was no way I was taking Jerrica back, either.

"No one said anyone was goin' back." Sting's voice startled me. I glanced sharply at the open door of the Bronco. He stood there, his big body silhouetted in the moonlight.

"I ain't goin' back either." Monica's voice wasn't as strong as Daisy's, but there was no doubt about her wishes.

"No, honey. You're not. We'll work it all out. Right now, we need to get back to the compound. Iris? You want to stay or ride with me?"

What kind of question was that? Of course, I wanted to ride with him! But little Clover's arms tightened around my neck, and I knew I couldn't leave the girls. Not even knowing they were safe.

Sting nodded once as if reading my mind. "I'll see you back at the clubhouse."

"But I didn't say anything."

"You didn't have to, hellcat. They need to feel safe. You're safe to them. No way you leave them when you know they need you." Strangely he didn't sound angry or resigned. He sounded... proud?

"You're right. I can't leave them."

"You're a good woman, Iris. You'll make a great ol' lady." Why would he say that? What did that even mean? "We'll get the young ladies settled. The women of the club will help with anything you need. Then we'll go find Brick and bring your sister home."

I needed to say something. To thank Sting or protest not going to get Jerrica now. Anything. But I nodded and wrapped my arms tighter around the girls. He was right. They needed to be taken care of.

"Will Brick take care of Jerrica?"

"He will until you get there. He'll protect her with his life."

"Why would he do that? He doesn't know us."

"Two reasons, hellcat. Brick is loyal to me. I told him to protect her with his life, so he will. Gladly. Second? He's not exactly what I'd call a good guy, but he's the most protective man I know. Even more than me. He will protect that girl with his life because she needs protecting."

I sighed. Brick was the strong, silent type. The really big strong, silent type. It was possible he would terrify Jerrica, but there was no help for it. The quicker they got these three girls settled, the faster she could get to Jerrica.

Atlas opened the driver's door and slid behind the wheel. "Let's get you four home."

"Ain't goin' back to the home!" Daisy sat up and tried to get out of the car.

"Relax, honey. Poor choice of words." Atlas tried to smooth things over. "I should have said your *new* home. Ain't no one there gonna hurt you. We got you away from the ones who took you. Besides, do you think Iris would let you go with us if it weren't safe?"

Daisy stopped, moving closer to me. "No." Her voice was soft now. Like she'd been chastised.

"Look, I get it." Atlas continued to turn in his seat. We couldn't see his face, but his voice was pitched low. I suspected he was trying to be soothing, but he wasn't built for it. Honestly, I wasn't sure the girls needed soothing. They needed to know they had strong protectors. "You don't know us. Right now, though, we're the best chance you've got. You can't go back to the group home, and you can't be out on the streets. You give the men and women at Black Reign twenty-four hours. They don't earn your trust, I'll personally take you anywhere you want to go. No questions asked."

"We ain't got nowhere to go." Monica's voice was little more than a whisper.

"You don't like it at Black Reign, I'll take you back with us to Iron Tzars." Sting's voice was as soft as Atlas's. It surprised me he made that offer. Which told me he was probably counting on the people at Black Reign to make things so good for them the kids didn't want to leave. It would be easy to do. They had children of their own in the compound, and they made a tight community who welcomed others willingly.

"I want to stay wherever Iris is." Monica hugged my middle tightly. "I promise I won't be no trouble. Can you adopt me like you're gonna do Jerrica?"

Sting interrupted before I could answer. I was thankful, because I had no idea what to say to the girl. "We'll talk about it tomorrow. Right now, the important thing is to get you inside the Black Reign compound where it's safe. Just hang on a little longer."

The girls didn't say anything, but I felt Monica nod even as she tightened her arms again. Clover didn't even whimper. I could feel her warm breath against my neck. She had something close to a stranglehold on me, but I wasn't about to tell her to ease up. The girl needed me. Same as the other two. Same as Jerrica.

There was no putting on seat belts, but Atlas was careful. Once we rolled inside the gates to Black Reign, he seemed to breathe easier. I know I did, and I had no idea why. Apparently, I'd come to recognize this place as a haven. The girls noticed too, because Daisy eased away from me and looked out the window. There were several men outside the building, but even more women. The wives and girlfriends of the members were out in force. They all looked anxious but waited until their men gave them the OK before surrounding the vehicle and helping the girls out.

"You ready, hellcat?" Sting helped me out of the vehicle. Jezebel took Clover who, surprisingly, went with her without a fuss. El Diablo wrapped another blanket around the little girl in his wife's arms and brushed one big hand down her tangled hair. I looked up at Sting, tears in my eyes, and nodded.

"Did you take care of those fuckers?" I didn't really want to know, but I needed to know. I needed to know what kind of man I was dealing with. If he'd let them go, it would break the attraction I felt for him. If he hadn't? Well, I wasn't sure what I'd do with that.

"We'll talk about it later. Your sister will need you once Brick has her."

"I thought he'd rescued her already." My heart rate skyrocketed. "I thought she was safe."

"By the time we get there, she will be. Let's go."

He led me to a motorcycle and handed me a helmet. "Put it on. When we get there you can ride with your sister. I'm sure she'll need you as much as you need her."

"I'm scared." Sting would never know what that admission cost me. I wasn't even sure why I blurted it out.

"I know, hellcat. This is where I earn your trust." He pulled me into his arms, and I stiffened. I wasn't used to affection, even from Jerrica. She thought she was too old for it, and maybe she was. But I craved it. I inhaled sharply. The sharp, masculine scent of sweat and gasoline should have been off-putting, but it wasn't. It was comforting in a way it never should have been. This was a man who worked. He did what he said. He got the girls away from the warehouse, and he had men he trusted getting Jerrica. When I looked up at him, he leaned down and brushed a kiss across my lips. Just like before, it sent butterflies loose in my stomach. He didn't do more than press his mouth to mine, but it was enough to make me crave more. The sensation was as unsettling as it was exhilarating.

When he pulled away, he looked straight into my eyes. "It'll be OK, Iris."

I nodded. For the first time in three months, I felt

like it might be OK. That was Sting. His charisma. I wasn't sure when I chose to believe him. It wasn't even a conscious decision on my part. But I believed him. I was all in, putting my hopes in the hands of a man I didn't know.

God help him if he couldn't deliver.

God help me.

Chapter Five
Sting

"Give me a rundown."

I sped down the road with Iris's arms around my middle. Inappropriate as it was, my cock responded to her proximity. Filing away thoughts of my little hellcat writhing under me in pleasure for after I got her sister back, I listened through my earwig while Wylde gave me an update. It was standard equipment on an operation like this, along with a tiny microphone clipped to my shirt.

"Jerrica is the only girl in this group. Not sure if the others were already sold, or if something else happened." Wylde sounded like he'd been through the wringer. He was good at his job, but he was in a strange place with strange people working with him. To say he didn't play well with others was the understatement of the century.

"Best guess?"

"They're dead. Still prudent to question those motherfuckers, though. If the girls ain't dead, I'd like to give Black Reign a place to start lookin' for 'em."

"Keep digging, Wylde. Get all the information you can. I'll see if Brick left anyone alive to question."

"He did. Though none of them are in good shape."

It was another half an hour before we made it to the rendezvous point. Brick had loaded up the bad guys and tied them inside the bed of the F-250 they'd brought along. Jerrica was in the back seat, huddled under a blanket. Iris opened the door, and Jerrica launched herself at Iris and sobbed uncontrollably.

"I'm here, baby. I'm right here." Iris was crying right along with Jerrica.

The two of them clung together, and my heart swelled. I'd kept my promise to Iris. Iris had kept her promise to Jerrica. I was sure the girl would have a lot of therapy or something to go to, but she was with her sister, and they were both safe. We'd figure out the rest.

Iris looked up at me. "Thank you, Sting. Thank you so much!"

"I'm here to slay your demons, Iris. I'll always be here." I could tell my words confused her. She looked over Jerrica's head and met my gaze, questions in her lovely eyes. There was no way I could not take her in my arms, even with her sister clinging to her. So I wrapped both of them up and let them lean on me.

Iris went willingly, one arm wrapped securely around Jerrica, the other around my neck. Jerrica stiffened and pulled away from me but retained her death grip on Iris.

"It's ok, baby." Iris smoothed Jerrica's matted, dirty hair away from her face. "I found him at Black Reign. They sent him and his crew after you."

"Told you, little badger. Promised I'd take you to your sister, and here she is." Brick stepped close and put another blanket around Jerrica's shoulders.

The girl looked back at Brick before addressing me. "You know Brick?"

"I do. I'm with your sister too."

She didn't acknowledge me but gave me a solemn look. "Brick saved me."

"We all did, honey." Brick's voice was gruff. "You've got a bunch of badass protectors now. You and your sister."

"Did you kill 'em?" Jerrica didn't look scared now. She looked... fierce.

"Not yet. I promised you we would, and we will.

Just want to get some information from them first."

"You promise? I want you to kill 'em."

Brick nodded once at Jerrica and knelt before her. He put one hand on her shoulder. "I promise, little badger. I'll make 'em suffer."

"Good." The child swiped her arm over her face, then put her chin up and turned back to Iris. "Can we go home now?"

"Yes, baby. We're going home."

"Wait!" Jerrica's eyes got wide, and she shook her head. "Not *that* home. I don't wanna ever go back there!"

"You're coming with us, Jerrica. You and your sister." I couldn't keep quiet any longer. The quicker Iris realized she was mine, the better.

"Back to Black Reign. Hope has been so worried about you." Iris continued to brush off streaks of dirt and strands of matted hair away from the child's face. "Everyone has."

"Back to Black Reign, then we'll talk, Iris." I spoke softly, not wanting to alarm Jerrica into thinking I'd put her in a bad situation. "You'll both be protected."

Iris gave me a wide-eyed look but didn't say anything else. I hoped she didn't think I intended to separate them, but now wasn't the time to discuss it. I met her gaze with a steady one of my own and hoped she understood.

I stood there, embracing both my charges. Roman pulled up in a Bronco Sport that was smaller than the one we'd used at the warehouse and a different color. I was glad to see he'd brought something for the girls to ride in, but I'd be damned if he was going to be the one to take them back.

When he got out of the vehicle, I jerked my head

in the direction of my bike. Roman nodded before taking charge of it. Normally, I'd never trust someone other than perhaps Brick with my bike, but there were more important things to consider. I wasn't leaving Iris and Jerrica with anyone. I was their protector. I'd be the one to see them back to the compound safely.

Iris and Jerrica clung together in the back seat. I noticed Iris had put her seat belt on and had pulled Jerrica's around her hips. The younger girl clung to Iris as best she could, her slender shoulders shaking as she cried silently. Several times during the ride, I met Iris's gaze in the rear-view mirror. Yeah, she was anxious. She kept rubbing her sister's back over and over, murmuring softly to her. Anyone could see they loved and needed each other.

The Bronco was flanked by the three bikes. The truck was farther back. Wrath was on standby in case we had any law trouble, but the farther away we could keep the girls from anything about to happen with these fuckers the better.

We rolled into the compound and didn't slow down. The prospects had the gate open and shut it the second we were inside. Rycks and Samson directed us to a garage at the back of the property. Iris still held Jerrica securely but looked around as we went deeper into the property.

The Black Reign road captain, Mechanic, promptly pulled every vehicle -- bike or cage -- into a garage, and several men descended on them with water and cleaning solution and lots of rags. By the time the man was finished with them, there wouldn't be a trace of anything that could point to us, the girls, or our cargo. They'd be clean as a virgin's honey pot.

"Nice work." Rycks held out his hand, and I took it. "You're welcome to be in on the interrogation if you want. This was your operation. We'll handle the cleanup. You go as far as you want. After that, El Diablo will finish with anything left of them."

"I got what I came for." I nodded in the direction of Iris and Jerrica. "How are the others?"

"Skittish. Though, the one called Daisy is demanding to talk with Atlas. She said she's not leaving Iris no matter how much she likes it here."

"If they want to come with us, I'm good with it. Though, I'm gonna need some legal way to keep them. I won't have social services or some shit hunting them down and trying to put them back into a group home. They don't need the stress, and I don't want Iron Tzars under that much scrutiny."

"You willing to be their guardians? Because Shotgun and Wrath can make a legal adoption happen."

"I'll talk with Iris. If she's good with it, I am. Ain't got another patched member at Iron Tzars who's married, though I can still see if a couple of them are willing to be guardians. Two of the older guys have kids around the same age, other than Clover. She's a little young."

"Talk to Iris. I can have them set something up ready to be executed after you get back to Evansville, but it would be better if we had it straightened out before you leave. No chance of accidents that way."

"Understood." I needed to get Iris and Jerrica back to their room so Iris could get the younger girl to sleep. Then she and I had some things to discuss. Not the least of which was her not trusting me and running off on her own. I fully intended to punish her for that.

"Lyric has the ol' ladies together. They've got the other girls with our daughters and a few puppies." Rycks grinned. "Nothing puts a female at ease like a puppy."

"I'll have Iris take Jerrica to them after Fury and Noelle check her out. The other girls get checked over?"

"Yeah. Surprisingly, other than some bruises and being a bit on the malnourished side, they're in pretty good health. Noelle said there was no evidence of sexual assault, and all three of them deny it."

"Thank God for small favors." I sighed. "I can't wait to get my hands on those motherfuckers."

"We're taking them to an interrogation room." He nodded in the direction of a wooded swamp area off in the distance. "Basement room. It's damp and not very comfortable, but it's also damned near impossible to find unless you know what you're looking for. Chief and Loki are waiting for them."

"Chief? Not *the* Chief."

Rycks grinned. "The one and only."

Chief was a legend in Black Ops and in the MC community. No one really knew how old he was, or where he came from. But he was of Native descent and not someone you wanted to cross. Ever.

"Fuck me. He gonna do this?"

"Only if you want him to. He and Loki were just going to soften them up. Though, Chief says your man Brick did a beautiful job."

"Brick isn't the most subtle of interrogators. He was givin' 'em a taste of what's in store for them."

"One hour good? You need more time?"

"Give me two. Iris and I have some things to discuss, then I'll be back. I'll see what I can get out of them, then let Chief have his way with them. Ain't really interested in much since my job was to retrieve the girls. You guys want us on the second part of the job, the shutting down the ring part, let us know.

Otherwise, I'm good to head back to Evansville first thing tomorrow."

"I assume Brick's gonna want a part in this too?"

"Yeah. He made a promise to Jerrica. Never known the man to go back on his word."

As if I'd summoned him, Brick stepped out of the shadows and next to us. "Promised that girl I'd make 'em suffer."

"Anytime you're ready, Brick." Rycks was all business. We could have been talking about the weather instead of having a discussion about torturing the men we had captive.

"I'll watch while Chief goes to work. Once I'm satisfied, I'll let him know."

"I say God help them, but they don't deserve any help. Do your worst, Brick. Chief will get any information he can get out of them, then you can have at 'em."

Brick nodded and headed to the building where Rycks had indicated they held the men. With a nod at me, Rycks followed Brick. I took a breath. Iris and I had a myriad things to discuss. First of which was the fact that she was mine, and I wasn't letting her go. The sooner she figured that out, the better.

* * *

Iris

I found the other girls in a suite on the second floor of the center building in the compound. They were cleaned up and looking much better than when I'd found them. Clover sat in Jezebel's lap with a fuzzy blanket, quietly watching while the other girls giggled around a table. They'd set it up with basins of water, washcloths and towels and various face creams including scrubs and masks, as well as a big case of high-end makeup.

Two enormous Saint Bernards sat on the floor watching everything around the girls. Every so often someone would reach over and scratch the head of one of the dogs. When she stopped, the dog would simply move to another girl at the table until someone started petting her again.

Every woman in the room I'd met at the Christmas party the month before. Some were married to men in the club, while others were their children. Dawn was Jezebel and El Diablo's daughter. She seemed to be the ringleader of the bunch, encouraging the young women in the group to try various things. It wouldn't have been something I'd have chosen to do, but everyone was all smiles, seeming to enjoy themselves.

Clover looked up at me and smiled. She pointed to the table.

"Hi, sweetie. No, I don't think I'll join, but Jerrica might want to."

Clover nodded vigorously and climbed down from Jezebel's lap, going to Jerrica and taking her hand with a pleading look. Jerrica looked back at me.

"Up to you, honey. Do you want to take a shower first?"

Jerrica nodded, squeezing Clover's hand. "I'll be right back. OK?" That was my sister. She was always looking out for those smaller than her. Clover in particular had taken up with Jerrica the last few months. Instead of letting Jerrica go do her thing, Clover kept hold of her hand as Jerrica went to the bathroom.

"You can stay with me if you want, Clover." I wanted my sister to have some privacy. I figured she needed it.

"It's OK. I don't mind if she stays with me." Jerrica saw the blanket Clover had been holding and picked it up, handing it to the younger child. Clover took it and rubbed the thing against her face with a smile. The blanket was obviously a source of comfort.

"Do you want me to go with you, honey? I can watch Clover while you shower."

"We'll be OK." She smiled down at Clover. "Won't we, kiddo?"

Clover smiled and wrapped her arms around Jerrica's middle in a fierce hug. Jerrica kissed the top of Clover's head.

"I've put some clothes on the vanity for you, Jerrica." Jezebel spoke softly. The girls at the table continued to do their thing. All of them acknowledged Jerrica's presence with waves but didn't stop what they were doing. Monica kept glancing at us but didn't offer to welcome Jerrica into their group even though they'd been friends before. I figured it was a mixture of uncertainty and knowing Jerrica had been gone far longer than any of them. They likely had no idea what to do or what to say to their friend.

"Thank you, Ms. Jezebel. You're always so nice."

"Honey, I'm only nice because you're even nicer. Ask anyone. I'm a badass." The older woman lifted her chin and gave Jerrica a cocky smirk, looking so much like all the men in the club I nearly burst out laughing myself. Jerrica laughed and ran back to the other women, throwing her arms around Jezebel.

"You're almost as wonderful as my sister." Jerrica's comment was so soft I almost didn't hear it.

"High praise indeed. Iris is a remarkable woman. I've gotten to know her over the last few months. I see why you love her so much."

Jerrica looked back at me. "She's the best big

sister in the world."

"You're the best little sister in the world." I grinned at her, trying to hold back my tears. "Go on. Get your shower so you can join the group."

Clover snagged Jerrica's hand again and led the way to the bathroom. Clearly the girl wanted Jerrica at that table with the others.

Once the door was closed, a hand landed gently on my shoulder. I looked back to find Sting right behind me. I knew he'd been there the whole time, but he'd allowed us to enter into the group in our own way. I doubt many men would have had the foresight for such a thing, but I was beginning to realize Sting wasn't an ordinary man.

"She'll need to be seen by the doc. Just like the others." His voice was gentle. I knew he was right, but I wanted to put it off as long as possible. I didn't want her to have to relive this any more than she had to.

"I know. I wanted her to feel normal for a while."

"Honey." Jezebel came to me and urged me and Sting out of the immediate vicinity. Once we were in the kitchen area, she spoke in hushed tones. "You know she's never going to be normal again. Right? We have no idea what happened to her yet, but we know what they were setting her up for."

"I probably shouldn't have suggested she shower. But after so long, I doubt they'd be able to collect DNA anyway."

"That's not something you need to worry about, Iris." Now, Jezebel had the look on her face I'd seen the men have. She was readying herself for battle. "DNA isn't going to make a damned bit of difference."

"But, won't the court need it when we go to trial?"

I looked from Jezebel to Sting and back. They

gave each other a grim look. Jezebel was the one to speak.

"There isn't going to be a trial, Iris. And I think you know that."

I sighed. "Yeah. Sorry."

"As long as you realize what's happening." Sting framed my face with his hands. "No one hurts my girls and gets away with it. Even if you weren't my girls when they took her, you are now."

"El Diablo doesn't let human traffickers live long in his territory," Jezebel said softly. "These guys were dead the second he found out they were in his area. Preying on those he considers his."

"What about Mr. Brown?" The sudden thought about the man who was supposed to protect all these girls nearly made me see red. My vision tunneled as my anger spiked. All I could see was his face as he callously told me he'd sent Jerrica off with strangers. There's no way he didn't know what he was doing.

"Iris? Take a breath." Strong arms lifted me. I thought I might need to fight someone off, but that comforting scent of masculine sweat and gasoline surrounded me, and I relaxed. And the tears came. "Come on, Iris. Breathe. In and out, baby. In and out."

"I'll get Fury." That was Jezebel.

I sucked in a breath. Then another one. "Sting..."

"I'm here, little hellcat. I've gotcha."

"I'm sorry. I'm sorry." Now that I'd broken through the panic, I trembled in Sting's arms. Looking up into his face, I saw nothing but understanding and a hint of satisfaction. That look finally broke through the rage and fear consuming me. I knew I'd probably made a fool out of myself so I tried to scramble out of his arms.

"No need to be sorry. That's what I'm here for."

He kissed the top of my head. "You good?"

"No! I'm not good! Sting, Mr. Brown is still at the home. What if he's planning on sending more girls away? He got three out after Jerrica, and no one even questioned him!"

"Relax, baby. Black Reign has something going with him. I ain't in their club, so I don't need to know about that. But he's not gonna hurt anyone else again."

"You promise?" I needed the reassurance even as my mind shied away from what would happen to the director of the home my sister and I had lived in for years. I didn't want that bastard free, but I wasn't sure I was ready to say I wanted him dead.

OK. That wasn't true. I did want him dead. I didn't want my hands dirty. How hypocritical was that?

"I swear it, hellcat. He's not gonna ever hurt anyone again."

I wound my arms around his neck and let loose a little sob. I didn't want to break down. Now wasn't the time. Jerrica would be out of the bathroom soon, and I needed to be strong for her. She had so much to deal with, and I needed to be with her. She needed to know she wasn't alone and that she had a strong protector. How could I be that when I was losing my mind at the moment?

It wasn't long before Noelle and Fury entered the room. Sting had taken me to a bedroom where he had finally calmed me down out of the view of the children. Fury stood back while Noelle took the lead.

"I think you're fine," she said with a smile. "Just a bit of an emotional release. Want us to look at your sister while we're here? You can stay with her if she wants, and we can do it in a non-clinical setting."

It was hard to focus, but I looked from Noelle up

to Sting. I have no idea why I did it, but once I did, he took over. I was surprised at how relieved I was. I didn't feel like I was capable of making any decisions at the moment.

"If Jerrica is comfortable with it, then yes. It will be better to get it over with so she can join the other girls and be a kid for a while."

"She needs a break the same as you do, Iris."

I nodded my head. "As long as she's OK with it."

"I'll be gentle when I ask her." Noelle gave me a genuine smile. I remember how she was with the other girls and knew Jerrica was in good hands.

It wasn't long before Noelle had Jerrica in the bedroom with us. Noelle had Fury and Sting step outside so she could talk with Jerrica and see any injuries she had.

"If I need Fury to look at an injury, I'll call him back in. Otherwise, he'll rely on my judgment. Should be easier on Jerrica."

Jerrica looked from me to Noelle. "It's OK, Iris." Then her gaze went back to Noelle. "As long as there ain't needles. I don't like needles."

"I'm not going to promise. Fury might want to do some blood work. Just not today. That I can promise."

Jerrica sighed and repeated, "I don't like needles."

"Want to know a secret?" Noelle leaned in close to Jerrica. "I don't like needles either."

"Really?" Jerrica's eyes got wide, and the ghost of a smile tugged at her lips. "You might be better'n I thought. I don't like doctors either."

"Well, then you'll love me. I'm not a doctor." Noelle reached a hand to Jerrica. "I'm an MMA fighter. I help because Fury's too scary. He looks like a meanie, but he's really a teddy bear."

That did get a small giggle out of Jerrica. I could have happily kissed Noelle. Jerrica needed to have someone look her over, but I couldn't have let anyone else make her submit to an exam.

Thankfully, Noelle didn't take long. It was just the three of us. When Noelle asked Jerrica the inevitable questions about sexual assault, I had to fight to hold back tears. Again, like with the others, Jerrica denied anyone touching her inappropriately.

"I wasn't really expecting it." Noelle brought Fury back to the room after Jerrica joined the other girls.

Sting nodded. "If they were going to sell her, they'd want her to be untouched. It would increase the price." He pulled me into his arms, kissing my temple. "You satisfied she'll be good for a while?"

Oh. That's right. He wanted to talk. "I won't leave without telling her where I'm going."

"Didn't expect you to. Tell her you'll come get her in the morning. Jezebel knows how to find us if she needs you."

I did as Sting said, reassuring Jerrica. She didn't want me to go, but Clover took her hand and led her to Jezebel, climbing up into the woman's lap. Jerrica looked back at me, then followed Clover, and the girls snuggled against Jezebel and each other. Noelle took a blanket from the back of the couch and wrapped it around the girls' shoulders. Jezebel spoke softly to them. Jerrica smiled once. Clover looked up at Jezebel and smiled before laying her head on Jezebel's shoulder and closing her eyes. Jerrica looked at me one last time and smiled.

"I promise I'll be here in the morning, honey."

"I know." Jerrica didn't look scared. Strangely, I

thought Clover's acceptance helped ease Jerrica's fear. "You sent Brick after me last time. You didn't forget me."

"I could never forget you, Jerrica. Not ever!"

She looked at Sting. "You gonna take us with you, or are we gonna stay here?"

"That's what me and your sister need to work out. Plannin' on takin' you with me. You good with that?"

"Will Brick be going too?"

"He's my vice president. He goes where I go."

"Then I guess it's OK if we go with you."

"You like Brick, huh?" Sting grinned. I got the feeling he was very pleased with Jerrica. "You know he's not the only one who can protect you. Right? I'm pretty handy myself."

"Yeah, but he's much bigger'n you. So he has to be better." I could tell Jerrica was only half joking. Brick made her feel safe like Sting made me feel like he could fix anything. Sting had brought Jerrica back to me. And the other girls I hadn't even known were missing. He'd never intended to leave them or Jerrica. He wasn't willing to risk their lives. So he found an alternate way of doing things.

"That he is, honey. That he is. So, you good for the night?"

"I'll be here with you and Clover." Jezebel smiled at the two girls. "We can build a blanket fort if you like."

"That would be fun." Jerrica grinned at Clover, and the girl nodded eagerly.

"Good. If you need Iris, just tell Jezebel, and she'll send someone after her. We'll be in the compound. We're not leaving. We need to talk."

Jerrica didn't need any other convincing. While

she probably had some pretty rough days and nights ahead, for now she was content. Whatever had happened when Brick rescued her, he'd made an impression. If it put her mind at ease, I was thankful they'd made a connection.

"Come on, little hellcat," Sting said, tugging my hand so I had to follow him. We've got a long night ahead of us."

Now, why did that simple statement send thrills through me?

Chapter Six
Sting

Having Iris in my room was more satisfying than I could have imagined. No, it wasn't really my room, but it was the space I'd been living in for the last three months. She eyed me warily, like she knew I was ready to pounce on her.

"Are you afraid of me, Iris?"

She shook her head. "No."

"Good. I see no sense in dragging out this part of the conversation. I want you and Jerrica to come with me back to Evansville. I'll get Wrath to make your adoption of Jerrica happen now instead of waiting on the state of Florida to make a decision."

Her lips parted. "You can do that?"

I shrugged. "Ain't my territory, but Wrath's a damned good lawyer. Besides that, he has Shotgun and Esther working with him. They can file the proper documents and get it pushed through in record time."

"As long as Jerrica comes with me, I don't care where we live. I need to be able to get a job to support us."

"Don't worry about that either. I'll take care of both of you. The club takes care of its own."

"The club. Your club?"

"Iron Tzars. Yes. I came here for advice from my father, Warlock. He was president of Iron Tzars until a month ago. I hadn't been here long when you came to Hope for help. El Diablo asked for our help with this. It's what we do. Shut down human trafficking rings when we find them."

"They have a lot of that in Indiana?"

"Not what I'd call a lot, but more than you'd think. We're not so naive to think we've shut them all down in the area, but we do what we can. They needed to find Jerrica fast. We did the best we could. Still took us three months."

"I might never have found her if you hadn't come along. Thank you, by the way. I'm sorry I doubted you."

"Which brings me to another part of the discussion. You're in trouble, little hellcat."

She took a step back, eyeing me with caution. "Trouble?"

"Don't act like you don't know what I mean. I promised you a spanking for running off on your own. I think it's time for me to follow through."

Iris tilted her head, managing to look both incensed and intrigued. "I'm not letting you abuse me, Sting. No matter how good you kiss."

"You like my kisses?"

She rolled her eyes. "You know I do."

"Before we start this, my name is Aiden Wagner. Call me whatever you're comfortable with, but you should at least know my name."

"Why would it matter to you if I know your name or not?"

I stepped closer to her. She didn't back up. Instead, she rested her hands on my chest, her gaze following her touch. I waited until she looked up at me again before I answered her.

"You're mine, Iris. Everyone in my club knows it. Everyone at Black Reign knows it. Since the moment I first saw you, I knew you were going to be mine."

She sucked in a breath, her eyes going wide. "What does that mean?" Her whispered question was followed by a shiver through her body. Her fingers clutched at my chest, and sweat glistened on her upper lip and forehead. Her pupils dilated, and she wet her lips, her gaze dropping to mine.

"Oh, I think you know what it means. Just to be clear, though, I'm makin' you my ol' lady. We'll *both* adopt Jerrica. It gives me the woman I've grown to admire over the last three months and gives you the protection you need for your sister and yourself. As the ol' lady of their president, my club will protect you with a ruthlessness you've never even conceived of. With Jerrica as my daughter, they'll be worse with her. She'll always have a strong protector with her. You won't have to worry about adopting her by yourself. I'll be your husband. We'll be a strong family unit for her."

"You don't know me. I don't know you. This isn't something we can do on a whim."

"This isn't a whim, Iris. Tell me you've not been studying me the three months we've been here together. Tell me you never noticed me as a man, and I'll forget about this."

She opened her mouth, then closed it. Stepping closer to me, she rested her forehead on my chest between her hands. "Fuck."

"That's what I thought. Now. We're not leavin' this room until we have this worked out between us. Tell me what expectations you have for a husband."

"You're too bossy for me." Her voice was muffled, but I thought I caught a thread of humor.

"Hellcat, you don't know the half of it. What else do you object to?"

She raised her head, looking me in the eyes. "I don't do casual sex. And I need to know what being an ol' lady means. 'Cause I don't share." Oh, she was a fierce little thing. I knew where she was going, and I loved her thinking.

"Being my ol' lady in my club is the same as

being married. I'll give you a nice ceremony and all that shit if you want. I'll even make it legal. But for all intents and purposes, me claiming you as my ol' lady means we're an exclusive couple. My club will enforce that in no uncertain terms. Neither of us will ever cheat on the other."

"What about a divorce? If you can just decide I'm your woman, can you decide you don't want me anymore?"

I shook my head. "It's more complicated than that. I let the club know what I want. They have to agree. Especially since I'm their president. They'll want to make sure we're a good match for each other. They've been judgin' us almost since the first day we met. Every member of Iron Tzars will report what they find to the other officers in the club, and they'll vote. If they agree, I'll get your property patch. Same with a divorce. The officers will listen to both sides and decide if we need to try harder to work it out or if we're done." There was more, but I wasn't about to tell her. Not now. It made me a bastard, but I needed her on board with this. Because there was no way I could let her go. She was under my skin but real fucking good. "You should know that I grew up in Iron Tzars. I'm twenty-nine. In all that time, I've never seen even one couple divorce. Warlock is the only man I've ever seen give up his ol' lady, and she wasn't approved by the club. He called her his ol' lady, but she wasn't really. The club knew they were a poor match. Or, rather, that she didn't want him. Not like he wanted her."

She looked up at me for a long time. I could almost see the wheels turning in her mind. In the three months I'd watched her, I knew Iris was nothing if not intelligent. Though I didn't want her to know there was no leaving the Tzars once she was on the inside, I had the feeling she could figure it out on her own.

"I know there are things you're not telling me. And I'm a fool for agreeing to this." She sighed. "What happens if we don't work out? I get the feeling I don't just get to go on my happy way."

"We'll work it out, Iris. I won't let it be any other way. I'll make you so happy, you'll never even think about leaving."

"You know that's just lip service. Right?"

"Is it? I made you a promise to get your sister back, and I did. I'm offering you the same kind promise on this. I'll keep you happy, Iris. I'll spoil you like a princess and treat you like a queen. Always, I'll keep you and your sister safe." I gave her a crooked grin. "And anyone else who comes along. Hopefully eight or ten boys."

Her eyes widened. "Eight or ten? You've lost your mind! And I am not having boys! Girls or nothing. Just to keep you honest."

Joy burst through me. I knew I had her. Pulling her into my arms, I hugged her tightly to me. "Honey, I'll be thrilled with any child you have. If we can't have kids, I'll be thrilled to have you all to myself once Jerrica grows up. Or we can adopt the girls in there with Jerrica. If not us, I know of several men who'd make great protectors for them. Starting with Brick."

"Right. I can see him playing Daddy to one of those girls. They'd mop the floor with him."

"See? You know more about us than you think if you've already got Brick pegged."

We grinned at each other for long moments. I smoothed back a strand of hair from her face. "So, what do you say?"

"You're not giving me long to decide, are you?"

I shrugged. "I give you too much time, you'll talk yourself out of it. Don't try to be logical about this. Trust your instinct. What does your gut tell you?"

She slid her arms around my neck, pulling herself up to brush her lips against mine once. "That I need more of your kisses. Desperately."

I took the opening she gave me. My arms tightened around her as I covered her lips with mine. Holding her close was imperative. The longer I kissed her, the more holding her close became a visceral need. I wanted us skin to skin, but that would have to wait. She had to be ready before I started ripping her clothes off.

Like before, the second my lips touched hers, magic happened. My body shot tight. My heart raced. My whole being was consumed with her. Iris. My woman. She opened her mouth to me, surrendering so sweetly my heart swelled. Then she dabbed her tongue against mine tentatively. As if testing the waters. Deciding if she liked the taste and feel of me.

She sighed and let me deepen the kiss. Her hands clutched my chest, and she held me as tightly as I held her. Fuck me, it felt *good*! I'd held her before, but never like this. Iris was mine. She was accepting me as hers.

When she moaned into my mouth, I swallowed her cries, wanting to keep them all. Every little thing about her, I wanted. Her courage. Her loyalty. Her love. I thought Iris had a capacity to love greater than any other woman I'd ever met. I knew my brothers saw it too. She'd make a wonderful ol' lady. More importantly, once I'd won her heart, she'd fulfill something in my life I never knew I was missing. Until I met her.

I lifted Iris into my arms, urging her to wrap her legs around my waist while I carried her to the bed.

With one arm securely around her back, I lay down on the mattress with her, my body solidly over hers as I settled us. When I pulled back slightly to look down at her, her eyes were glazed, and she had a beautiful smile on her face. It struck me then how little I'd seen her smile since we met. I had a feeling that, when I finally coaxed a full, joyous smile onto her face, I'd be gobsmacked by her beauty.

"I know I don't deserve you, Iris. But I swear to you, I'll make you happy. I'll do everything in my power to see you have the best life of anyone ever born from this point forward." I stroked the line of her cheek with the pads of my fingers. "Give me the chance to prove to you I can."

She took a breath. I could see the exact moment she decided to throw all in. Her face relaxed, and that soft, breathtaking smile took over her face. It was as lovely a sight as I'd ever seen.

"I'll follow where you lead, Aidan. But I'm telling you now, I want my sister with me. I promised her I'd adopt her, and I intend to keep that promise."

"Never thought about not including her in this. She'll have the benefit and protection of two parents, though. You'll marry me legally. We'll both adopt her. The others want to come with us. If you don't want to take them in, Iron Tzars will place them within the club. No matter who they end up with, they'll always be protected and spoiled. They deserve it after everything they've been through."

"No. I can take them."

"*We* can take them, Iris. Start thinking of us as a team."

She nodded, smiling up at me again. "I can do that."

"Good. I'll send word ahead. The club will have

a suitable place for all six of us ready when we get there. It will be a challenge in a short period of time, but we'll start work on a bigger place the second we get back."

"I'm not going to ask how these clubs seem to have all the money and resources in the world. I always thought motorcycle clubs met in dirty garages with grease rags all over the place and women hanging off them like fashion accessories."

That got a bark of laughter out of me. "Ain't sayin' there ain't women at the club, hellcat. Just that I have no intention of havin' anything to do with them. And if anyone had grease rags anywhere they weren't supposed to be in Clutch's garage, he'd beat their ass and no one would ever find the body."

"Who's Clutch?"

"He's our road captain. In charge of all things mechanical in the garage. He runs a tight ship."

"Good to know."

"Now. You ready to seal this deal?"

She grinned. "If by sealing the deal you mean you're going to fuck me now, then yeah. I want this so much I can't think of anything else."

That was all the encouragement I needed. Raising myself up slightly, I grasped the back of my shirt between my shoulders and pulled it off, tossing it onto the floor. I was rewarded with her slight gasp. Her lips parted and her gaze fastened to my chest. I knew what I looked like. I was muscled and tattooed, my body honed in the fires of battle. I was big and powerful. She was small and delicate.

Again, her hands landed on my chest. This time, she caressed the skin of my pecs up to my shoulders and down my arms. Her light touch feathered over me, and I had to resist the urge to rub against her hands like a contented cat.

Iris lifted herself up to place kisses over my chest. Her touch was light, little butterfly kisses everywhere she went. The sensations she created with such little effort drove me mad. She wasn't practiced, just curious. Perhaps even a touch nervous. I thought she might be trying to find her footing. Testing me. Trying to see what I'd let her do. I knew her experience had to be limited, so I contented myself with letting her get to know my body. We'd get to the heavy stuff later. We still had a good hour before I had to meet El Diablo and Chief in the interrogation room. Not an eternity, but enough time to let Iris play to her heart's content.

"First of all, let's get one thing straight." When she raised an eyebrow, I continued. "I ain't gonna fuck you this first time." When she opened her mouth to say something, I stopped her by kissing her thoroughly. I needed to remember that. The woman would argue with me all the time. This was the best way to shut her up when I needed to make a point. When I ended the kiss, she had a slightly dazed expression on her face. It was a good look on her. "I'm doin' this right, Iris. This first time is about me getting to know your body. I'm gonna pet and taste you. Gonna find out what you like. You're gonna sit back and let me play. Get me?"

She blinked up at me, trying to clear her mind. I could see her trying to shake off the lust riding her. "But what about you? I want you to enjoy --"

Again, I cut her off with a kiss, thrusting my tongue inside her mouth to lap. "I'm gonna enjoy the shit out of it, honey. Been wantin' this since the first time I saw you."

"Oh..." Her eyes got wide, like she was shocked.

"What? You didn't think I noticed how fuckin' sexy you were? You might have been distressed, but you went for what you wanted and made everyone listen to you."

"I was afraid they wouldn't believe me. The police didn't."

"Then you had to go and take off when you thought I wasn't movin' fast enough." I shook my head with a sigh.

She lifted her chin. "You said you were gonna spank me for that."

"So I did. And I will. Not yet, though. I want you to think about it. Wait for it. Anticipate it." She shivered and gave a small whimper. "Ah. I see that might be the very thing to do."

"Please, Aiden." Her plea was a mere thread of sound. "How can you make me feel like this so easily?"

I grinned. "Tell me how you feel, hellcat. Talk to me."

"I can't do that!" She sounded so outraged I had to chuckle.

"Sure you can." I leaned down and whispered at her ear. "Tell me how your pussy aches. Tell me how wet you got thinkin' about me spankin' your bare ass. Then tell me you want me to fuck you while I'm spankin' you."

That got a sharp cry and a full-body shiver from her. Her skin erupted in sweat. "Sweet God... What are you doing to me?"

"Gettin' you ready for me, hellcat. Gonna make you mindless before I take you. Then we'll see how high I can drive you before you come around my fuckin' cock." Again, she shivered, her legs tightening around my waist as she instinctively rubbed herself against me to get friction on her clit.

"I need to be naked," she whimpered. "*You* need to be naked!"

"You a virgin? Last thing I wanna do is hurt you."

Again, she looked up at me with wide eyes. "I've been too busy to form relationships. Should I have taken time?"

OK, that wouldn't do. So, I kissed her again. It was going to be my go-to for resetting her mind. Mainly because she tasted delicious. "Honey, I'm not gonna hurt you. Not for any reason. You're gonna get nothin' but pleasure out of this. If you're a virgin, I know I gotta be extra careful with you. If you're not, I still gotta be careful, but I know I won't hurt you once I get you wound up."

She took her time answering, looking away for several seconds. The urge to make her look at me was strong, but she needed to work this out herself.

Finally, she looked back. "Do you remember when you kissed me that first night?"

"Of course, I do. Sweetest lips I'd ever tasted. And you responded so beautifully I knew you loved it as much as I did."

I had to strain to hear what she said next. Took me a moment to realize exactly what she'd said. When my brain finally registered her words, my cock shot hard as fuckin' iron.

"Well, that was the first time I'd ever been kissed."

"Fuck... me..." There was no way to keep the silly grin off my face. Or the fact that my cock was hard as a motherfucker. I ground it against her, and she whimpered. "Feel that, hellcat?" When she nodded, her eyes wide and starting to glaze with lust, I rocked my hips from side to side. "That's what your confession did to me. I'm gonna be the only man in the entire fuckin' world to ever taste you. The only man to put my cock inside you. The only man to *ever* put his cum inside you. I'm gonna do all those things and make you love every blisterin', fuckin' second of it."

She cried out again, and this time she rocked her hips more aggressively. She must have found what she needed because a moment later, she screamed, her eyes flying open as her legs tightened around me. Her body convulsed with her orgasm. Judging by the way her gaze clung to mine in sweet confusion, she'd never done this herself before. Which made me grin all the more. Fuck. Yeah.

When she stilled, I lay on top of her fully, wrapping my arms around her tightly while I nuzzled her neck, praising her and trying to let her come down softly. "So sweet. So good. That's it, little hellcat. Just ride it out."

"Aiden." She whispered my name in a shaking voice. I kissed her jaw and cheek before settling on her lips again. I let the kiss go on for a long time. Just enjoying the sensation. I also wanted to bring her up again. Before I left this bed, I was going to give her as much pleasure as I could possibly manage.

The second she started to become an active participant again, I moved off her. "Let's get you undressed, hellcat. I'm fixin' to worship your body until I have to go meet with El Diablo and Chief. Then I'll come back and worship you again."

She nodded several times. "Yes! Let's do that!"

I chuckled, kissing her once before sliding her pants down her slender hips. I left her panties on because, Goddamnit, I wanted to take my time. Got her shirt off and the bra followed. I was not wasting any time getting to her tits. My mouth watered for the small mounds. Her rosy nipples stood out in stiff peaks. She groaned and tried to cover herself.

Naturally, I stopped her.

"Don't cover yourself, baby. I wanna see every fuckin' inch of your beautiful body."

She swallowed but put her arms back to her sides, though she did clutch the cover. I still had my jeans on, which I needed to remedy, but I knew the second my cock was free I'd want to sink into her and lose myself. I wasn't ready for that yet. *She* wasn't ready.

I leaned down and took one puckered peak between my lips, laving my tongue over it gently. She whimpered and squirmed under me. That was when I realized I was growling, and my eyes had slid shut. I glanced up at her. Couldn't tell if she was in pain or riding the edge of lust and madness. It was the only thing that made me focus on what I was doing when I hadn't even realized I'd already lost myself in her. And I wasn't even inside her yet!

"Shhh, baby," I crooned as I stroked her hair, trying to soothe her. "Am I hurting you? Are you comfortable?"

"No, I'm not comfortable!" I stilled. If I'd hurt her, I'd never forgive myself. I hadn't done anything but suck her nipple. Had I drawn on her too hard? "What are you doing to me? I'm on fire!" She was panting now, little breathless gasps that didn't seem like they gave her any real air. Almost like she was having a panic attack.

"Talk to me, hellcat. Tell me what to do. Am I scaring you? Do we need to stop?" I was alarmed now. I never wanted to scare her. Not for any reason.

"Don't you dare stop! Don't you fucking dare!" She tunneled her fingers through my hair and gripped. Hard. The pressure on my scalp told me she might have pulled more than a few strands of hair loose.

Instead of pushing me away, she pulled me closer, holding me to her breast. I wanted to chuckle, but I was so relieved all I could do was latch on and suck.

"I need something, Aiden. But I don't know what it is!"

"I got you, baby. You keep expressin' yourself any way you can. You figure out what you want me to do, say so. Otherwise, I'm listenin' to your sweet cries to guide me."

Iris seemed to shiver continually as she writhed beneath me. She said she'd never been kissed before. That meant it was doubtful she'd ever been touched by a man in a sexual manner. Which meant every sensation she felt now was sharp, something her body had never before experienced. Which meant she would be on sensory overload soon. If she wasn't already. That was where I wanted her. Madness.

After lavishing attention on both breasts, I kissed my way down her body. At first, she resisted, tugging my hair to get me back on her tits. When I trailed my lips down her belly, though, she froze. Her hand was still in my hair, but she let me move without resistance.

"What are you doing?" She'd started to hyperventilate again. Her panties were still on, so I had to peel them off her.

I sat up long enough to slide them down her shapely thighs. I started to toss the panties to the floor but paused, holding the simple lace undergarment in my hand, and stared at it. The compulsion couldn't be fought, so I brought it to my nose and inhaled. Her sharp, musky scent sent a punch of lust to my dick. There was no fucking way I was gonna last.

She stilled when I looked back at her. She was like a wild little deer, afraid of the headlights but afraid to move out of the way. I knew I needed to tone it down. Hard as it was. If she feared this act between us, she'd never recover from it.

"I'm good, hellcat." My voice betrayed me. I really wasn't good. I was on fucking fire! "I swear I'm not gonna hurt you."

"I know. Just... what comes next? Are you... are you gonna fuck me now?"

"Not yet, baby. And I already told you. This ain't fuckin'. I'm gonna take it nice and slow. Until I can't. So you have to tell me to ease up if I get too rough. I'm gonna fuckin' make love to you. Even if it fuckin' kills me!" I knew I sounded more harsh than sexy, but she didn't seem to mind. She smiled one of those beautiful, perfect, brilliant smiles of hers. I hadn't seen many, and none like this.

"I will. Just give me a warning before you, uh, you know. Put it inside me."

"Ain't gonna sneak up on ya, honey. Like I said. I refuse to hurt you."

"I've never had sex before, Aiden. Isn't it supposed to hurt the first time?"

"Honey, I'm a guy. I got no clue. But I refuse to believe I can't keep you from hurting if I take my time and go as slow as I'm able. You're worth any extra effort. Besides," I grinned at her, "Takin' my time prolongs my pleasure too. Now. You ready for me to keep goin'?"

"Are you kidding me? I've been ready this whole time! What the fuck, Sting?" Her brow furrowed in indignant confusion, and I couldn't help but laugh. I loved that she called me Aiden. This reversion to my road name made her all the more priceless.

"My God, what a fuckin' life we're gonna have together, hellcat." That made her whimper. I loved that she wasn't in control of her emotions. She was all over the place. The predominant mood seemed to be frustration and lust, but there was a healthy dose of need and vulnerability. I thought there might be a hint of something else too. Maybe she felt more for me than she was willing to admit. I'd get her there.

I kissed the tender flesh above her mound. A downy thatch of dark curls tickled my chin. Good. Because I doubted she could handle this without some kind of buffer. She was already on the edge. "I love how responsive you are, hellcat. You keep giving me that, and we'll have a fuckin' blast."

When I lowered my head farther, swiping my tongue through her folds, two things happened. First, Iris came unglued. She screamed and bucked, unable to decide if she liked it or not judging by the way she moved. She'd try to get away from me, then grip my hair and pull me back to her. She was a fucking wild thing under me! Second, I lost my Goddamned mind. Her sweet taste, the musky scent of her arousal combined with her uninhibited reactions set off every Alpha instinct in me. I wanted her writhing just like she was, but I had a primal need to hold her still for whatever I wanted to give her.

With a growl, I covered her pussy with my mouth, plunging my tongue inside her. If I'd thought she was confused before, this time she fought me like the hellcat I'd called her. I had to really pay attention to her to determine how much was overstimulation versus any real objection. She thrashed beneath my touch, digging her heels into the mattress and pushing away. I looped my arms around her thighs to hold her still, but I needed to make sure she was OK.

"Talk to me, Iris. You scared?"

She looked at me with wild eyes, like she wasn't sure where she was or what she was doing. "I -- what?

Why'd you stop?" There was a bite to her question and a flash in her eyes. Making her talk to me seemed to ground her and let her body catch up with her mind. Or maybe it was the other way around. Her body responded wonderfully. I thought maybe her mind got scrambled, and her instinct was to get away. It made sense when she was trying to take on adult responsibilities at such a young age. Which made me all the more determined to make sure she enjoyed herself.

Then it hit me. "Uh, Iris." I couldn't believe I'd forgotten about this. She clawed at me, pushing my head away, then pulling me closer. "Iris!" Her eyes snapped open, her pupils dilated. She was a woman lost in her own pleasure, and I felt like a fucking idiot.

"What's wrong? What'd I do?"

"Nothin', baby. You didn't do anything wrong. This is all on me. I need to ask you a question. I need your full attention, and you have to be completely honest with me." She stared at me blankly. Her eyes started to glisten with tears, and I felt doubly like shit. "Don't do that, baby." I brushed a finger at the corner of her eye and a tear slipped free. "I need to ask you a question, and I need you to be completely honest with me." She nodded slightly. "You good? You back with me?"

"I was always with you."

"No, baby. You were lost in pleasure. Right where I wanted you to be. But I can't continue until I know when your birthday is."

She blinked up at me. "What? You need to know this now?"

I scrubbed a hand over my face, still retaining my hold on her thighs. I could smell her arousal. Could still taste her sweet pussy. Could I really give this up after being so close to making her mine?

"Honey, tell me when your birthday is. It's important."

I could see the exact moment when she realized what I was talking about. Her eyes got wide and her lips parted. Florida's consent laws said eighteen was legal. They also allowed for someone who was sixteen or seventeen to engage in sexual activities with someone no older than twenty-three. A so-called Romeo and Juliet law. At twenty-nine, I was way outside that law, which meant I'd already gone too far if she hadn't turned eighteen.

"What's today?" When I just looked at her, she got an impatient expression on her face and huffed out a breath. "I've been so worried about my sister I didn't keep up with it!"

"It's March seventeenth, honey."

She sighed and smiled. "I turned eighteen three days ago. I'd offer my ID, but I'm naked, and it's in my room."

"Fuck." I let out a breath I hadn't realized I'd been holding. I was so light-headed with relief I saw spots for several seconds as I rested my head on her belly.

"What? I'm legal!"

"You are, baby. You totally are." I chuckled at my own relief. "Damned good thing too because I'm not entirely sure I could have stopped myself if you weren't."

"I'm not entirely sure I could have stopped myself from killing you if you did stop. Like you've already done." Her tone was snippy. Her red cheeks told me she was embarrassed. Not sure if it was because of how much she wanted this -- and I knew she did -- or because she'd forgotten her own birthday.

That I'd make up to her. Later.

"Well, I have no intention of fallin' into an early grave." I kissed her lower belly again before taking another swipe through her folds. She gasped but kept her gaze fixed on me. Yeah. I got it. I'd spooked her. Pulled her out of the moment one too many times.

"Fuck." I kissed her belly again before crawling up her body and settling my weight between her thighs. I found her mouth with mine and kissed her for long moments. My cock was hard as fucking steel and weeping with the need to come. But I wasn't coming anywhere but deep inside her.

This wasn't going the way I intended this to go. It was my own fault for not securing all the information I needed before I fucking started. But, by God, I wasn't stopping now. My dick found her entrance, and I eased the tip inside her before stopping. I didn't push inside, just let the sensations wash over me.

"This is it, hellcat. You ready?"

Wonder spread across her face. Eyes wide, her breathing rapid, she nodded. "I feel like I've been ready for this my entire life, Aiden. I've been ready for you."

That was all the encouragement I needed. Nodding once, I held her gaze as I slid inside her. There was no look of discomfort on her face, only that beautiful look of amazement. She reminded me of a child in that moment. I suppose she was in many respects. She'd been working for the better part of her life to be an adult. One capable of taking care of her sister when neither of them had anyone else. In doing that, she'd missed out on the joys of becoming an adult. All she knew was the labor. It was up to me to show her the fun of it.

With great care, I withdrew before moving forward again. In and out. In. Out. The longer I moved, the wider her eyes got. That overwhelming pleasure she'd been feeling before was returning to her. Doing everything in my power to coax her back to the brink, I kissed Iris as I moved inside her. Every stroke seemed to pull her deeper under my spell. Right where I wanted her.

It wasn't long before she was panting and sweating. Just like she had been before. She clawed at my back, digging her nails into my skin like little kitten claws. Her heels dug into my ass, pulling me to her more and more aggressively until I had little choice but to bend to her wishes.

"Aiden!" She gasped my name, her body tensing and moving erratically. She thrashed her head from side to side before finally arching her back and screaming at the top of her lungs. Her pussy spasmed around me. Until that moment I'd been concentrating on her so much I hadn't realized how close I was to coming. Her cunt milking me was all I could take. I let go, gritting my teeth and grunting as I shuddered above her. Just like I intended to, I pumped her full of my cum. We hadn't talked about it, but I didn't regret it even a little bit.

Iris… was *mine*.

Chapter Seven
Sting

I left Iris sound asleep in my bed. The sight filled me with more satisfaction than I could ever remember. I'd cleaned us both up before crawling back into bed with her and pulling her tightly against me. She asked if I'd come in her but had only nodded when I told her I had, and that I intended to come in her every fucking time I made love to her. She'd tried to hide her grin, but I'd seen it. She might have some reservations, but I was pretty sure they were mostly instinct. Rather, the way she thought she should feel about our relationship and the sex we'd shared. After that, she'd kind of passed out. One second she was smiling up at me, the next she slept like the dead.

I wanted to be back there with her now so I could wake her up in another couple of hours to do it again. Also, I was acutely aware I still owed her a spanking. Just the thought of that got me hard as a motherfucker. Now wasn't the time for those thoughts. In a chair in the middle of the room, four men sat tied soundly. They were beaten and bloodied, but not bad off. Yet.

"Ah, Sting. So glad you could join us." El Diablo gave me a cocky, knowing grin. Hell, the whole of the compound had probably heard us. It wasn't exactly like we were quiet. I didn't want her to be quiet, because if I could make her scream, I knew I was doing my job. Lord knew with her being eleven years younger than me I had to keep her satisfied. At least, that's how I looked at it. That meant keeping her uninhibited during sex.

"I'd say I wouldn't miss this for the world, but I won't lie. I'd much rather be up there with my woman."

"You don't have to be here if you don't want to be. Your vice president can handle your end." That was a genuine suggestion with no malice intended.

"Much as I want to, no. I need to be here for this. At least for a while."

Then the old El Diablo was back, smug as ever. "Have you at least, how do they say it? Locked her down?" Smug bastard knew exactly "how they said it." He was being a bastard.

If he thought he was going to get a rise out of me, he'd be wrong. "Damned straight I locked her down. That woman's mine. Wrath and Shotgun are working on the proper paperwork. By the time we're ready to leave, she'll be my wife, and those girls will be our daughters."

"So she agreed to take them on? Jezebel says they're insisting on going with Iris wherever she goes from here."

"She more than agreed to it. Besides, even if she didn't think she could handle it, we'd still take them with us and find a home for them in Iron Tzars. Got plenty of men willin' to take take on the role of father to those girls. And I mean that in the most respectable sense." I looked at the men getting ready to spill all they knew before they died. One of them looked like he was ready to kill us. One looked resigned to his fate. The other two looked scared shitless. Did my heart good. "You know. On second thought, I'm right where I want to be."

"That's the spirit." El Diablo rubbed his hands together like he was eager to get started. Given the maniacal gleam in his eye, I believed it.

The interrogation didn't take long. The two pussies sang like canaries, giving names and locations the second we took the tape off their mouths. The pissed-off one thrashed and yelled behind the tape, probably threatening the two with death or some shit.

"You don't get it, do you?" Chief said in his lightly accented English. I had no idea what nation of natives he belonged to, but Chief was the real deal in all respects. "It's not a matter of *if* any of you are going to die. You are. Your threats to hurt them are empty because you're going to die too." The big man drew his knife and casually made a slow cut down the guy's face. He cried out, but the tape held. Wonderful stuff, Duct Tape. "It's a matter of how soon you die." He nodded at the two men giving us the information we wanted. "They will die soon, but it will be a quick, clean death. You?" He shook his head solemnly. "Not so much. There is much evil you're responsible for, and you must pay your due."

Chief made another slow, deliberate cut, this time down the center of the guy's chest. Again, the guy screamed in pain. Blood flowed from the open wound in a bright crimson streak. Chief laid down his knife and picked up another blade. This one lay in the coals of a brick oven. Again, with slow deliberate movements, so the guy knew what was going to happen. He positioned himself so the knife hovered over the cut Chief had just made.

Chief grinned up at the man. "This may sting. Just a little."

He pressed the flat of the blade to the cut. Again, the guy screamed. This time it was higher pitched as the wound cauterized. The scent of searing flesh filled the room in all its gruesome glory. The two men cooperating whimpered and watched in horrified fascination, unable to look away.

When he was done, Chief turned his black gaze to them. "You're doing well. Please continue to do so."

The eeriest part about the whole exchange was the casualness with which Chief delivered his torture. There was no expression on his face whatsoever.

After El Diablo and Chief were convinced the two had given all the information they had, Chief gave them the quick end he'd promised by slitting their throats. We watched as they bled out. It took about thirty seconds or so. Not an instant death, but quicker than the other two were going to get.

Brick took over from there. Just as he'd promised Jerrica, he made them suffer. Together, he and Chief skinned both men alive. They weren't any more guilty than the other two, but follow-through was everything. It caused both of them to give us a few more pieces to our puzzle, including how Mr. Brown had traded girls at the home where Iris and Jerrica lived for silence on the embezzling he was doing from the fund Black Reign had set up for kids leaving the home to get an education in college or trade school, or to have something to start out life on their own with. That man would get more of what was happening here very soon. May he rot in hell alongside these scum.

"I think that will do," El Diablo said in his clipped accent. "I have what I need. I'll get the information to Giovanni and let him take it from there."

Rycks raised an eyebrow. "Not Shotgun?"

"Not this time. This is above his pay grade, so to speak. The men I'm looking for are better left to the Shadow Demons. They can take care of the bigger problem. All I want is for these scum to be out of my region. I think that problem is currently solved. Shotgun will ensure it stays solved."

"Good. With this business all done but the cryin', I'm goin' back to my woman. I don't want her to wake up without me." I was done with this shit. "Besides, these motherfuckers aren't worth another second of my time. Brick, I need your help with an internal matter." Brick would know exactly what I was talking about. "El Diablo, I'll need to ask for a favor when Brick and I are through."

The other man raised an eyebrow. "A favor?"

"Of the disappearing variety." It was all I was giving him for now. The affairs of Iron Tzars were our business. But I needed this done now. Before we headed back to Indiana with my woman and our children.

"I see. You can bring your problem back here if you like. We can dispose of it along with these."

I glanced at Brick, needing his opinion on this. When he nodded, I knew I was doing the right thing. "I'd appreciate that." I stepped over to El Diablo and stuck out my hand. "Allies?"

The man grinned. "Always. I'll look forward to collaborating with Iron Tzars in the future. I also appreciate the help on such short notice."

"Well worth any inconvenience, El Diablo. It got me my woman."

"She'll be a good ol' lady for you, Sting. Take good care of her."

Normally I'd snap that it wasn't any of his fucking business how I treated my woman. In this case, however, it was said as a reminder that what I'd been given by the universe was very precious. I couldn't fault the man for that. "I intend to. You keep your woman happy. She was instrumental in making all the girls feel safe. She's a remarkable woman. Besides, I have the feeling she'll cut you in your sleep if you don't."

El Diablo chuckled. "Yes. She would. But I keep

her happy because it pleases me to see her smile. I'd be shitty at my job if I couldn't fend off one small woman."

"Ain't sure I'd lump your woman in the same category as any small woman. She has a vicious streak anyone can see. If I were you, I'd rather not test it."

"Never worry on that account. I never intend to give her a reason to want to kill me in my sleep."

I grinned. "Good to know."

Brick and I went outside. I took a much-needed deep breath. It was good not to smell the metallic tang of blood in the air for a few minutes.

"I'll bring him here." Brick knew what to do. I could see in his gaze he approved of my decision. He looked away before saying, "Proud to be your VP, Prez. Your daddy was a good president. Until he wasn't. You're gonna be better." With that, he left for the compound.

Ten minutes later, he returned with Snake. Both men rode their bikes. Snake looked like he didn't have a care in the world. The man obviously didn't see any reason to fear me. I'd have thought he would have more respect for Brick though.

"Sting. Glad you're back from your foray."

I ignored his attempt at conversation. "We have a matter to clean up. Come with me."

Snake shrugged and followed me down the steps leading to the basement interrogation room with Brick following him. I opened the door and stepped inside where the bodies of the men we'd tortured were still in the chairs we'd secured them to. Chief stood in one corner, Black Reign's witness to the events going on inside their compound.

"I see you've been busy. Found the traffickers?"

"This isn't your concern, Snake."

He spread out his arms, giving me an impatient, amused look. "Then why am I here?"

"It's not going to work out with you in Iron Tzars. There can be only one president and you're not ever going to be it." I had no desire to drag this out.

"Well, I ain't leavin', pup. Iron Tzars is my life. I've been there for the better part of thirty years. I've put in my time. I'll be happy to stay out of club business if you want, but I'm not leaving my home."

"No." I said softly. "You're not leaving. No one leaves Iron Tzars."

Snake's eyes narrowed before he snorted and hiked a thumb back at Brick. "That why you brought your VP? To do me in?" He gave me an evil grin. "Got news for you, pup. Brick and I go back a long fuckin' way. He's not gonna take me out. No. You wanna do this, you'll have to do it yourself. And best of luck getting through Brick to do it."

I gave him a long, hard look before holding my hand out to Brick. The big man pulled out a wicked-looking serrated knife and laid it hilt-first in my hand. He put one hand on Snake's shoulder, squeezing tightly.

Snake's eyes widened, and his head whipped around to Brick. "What the fuck, Brick?"

"You know the rules. You also know I don't bend them for anyone. You challenged the president of Iron Tzars in front of everyone. He has no choice but to do this. You know he doesn't."

"If he knows he's in the right, why didn't he do it at the time of the infraction? No matter what he does to me, he still looks weak because he waited. Now he'll look indecisive *and* weak." Snake turned back to me, pointing a finger at my chest. "Mark my words, pup. Your days as president of Iron Tzars are numbered. No matter what you do here."

"He didn't kill you because he was angry. The president doesn't make permanent decisions when he's emotional." Brick's words were a soft growl. "It's why he'll be president for a very long time to come."

Brick stepped back, and I lunged forward, taking Snake in the kidney with my knife. I stabbed him over and over in quick succession before stepping back. Snake didn't cry out in pain, just looked at me with a kind of shock. Like he truly didn't think I had the balls to retire him. I watched until he died, never regretting my actions.

"Iron Tzars might have been your home, motherfucker," I said softly, "but it's my family."

* * *

Iris

I woke screaming as the mother of all orgasms crashed through my body. The covers were off, and Sting was once again between my legs with his mouth fastened to my pussy. His hungry growls would have amused me if I'd been able to form a coherent thought. As it was, I lay there and rode out wave after wave of pleasure. Once the wave started to ebb, I reached for Sting and pulled him over me.

"Good morning, hellcat." His grin was positively wicked. "You ready to start a new day?"

"With you? Always." I know I sounded like a satisfied cat the way I purred for him, but hey. Orgasms for breakfast needed to be on the menu every morning.

He kissed me, thrusting his tongue deep before his cock nudged at my entrance. With a groan, he sank into me in a slow, wet glide. I whimpered but arched to meet him. I might be new to sex, but this felt too fucking good to demure away from. If he wanted it, I was willing.

"I love the way you fit around me, Iris. Love the way you come for me."

"Sting..." I smiled as he continued to kiss me. God, I loved this! Though I'd just come my brains out, I could feel the wave rising again. My lower body tingled with every brush against my clit. "I'll never get enough of you. Never."

"Hot little thing. When we get home, I'm gonna spend the next week makin' love to you. Might even get around to that spankin' I promised you."

I giggled. "If I say I'm looking forward to it, will you still do it?"

In response, he flipped me over to my belly and sank back into my pussy. Then he whacked my ass with his hand. It stung, but the sensations seemed to morph into the most intense pleasure in seconds. I gasped, looking back over my shoulder. He smirked at me.

"That answer your question, hellcat?"

I narrowed my eyes. "Bet you won't do it again."

His lips parted in surprise. Then he gave me a positively evil grin. "Oh, baby. It's on."

The next half hour was quite possibly the best experience of my life. I found out my man would indeed do it again. In fact, I was pretty sure I wouldn't be able to sit down for a week. But it was *so* worth it!

"You good, hellcat? I didn't take it too far, did I?"

"This is the part where I'd normally reply with, 'If you have to ask...' but I can't. Because I loved every *blistering* second of it." I grinned at him over my shoulder. "See what I did there."

He threw back his head and laughed. I was glad of it, too. I knew he'd had to do some pretty horrific things the night before. He hadn't talked about it, and I hadn't asked, but I could see the hardness in his eyes. If I could erase that look for even a few minutes, I'd do anything it took.

"I see what you did, little hellcat." He kissed me once before getting up. "Come on. Shower, then we leave. I want to head out in thirty minutes."

"What about the girls?" I had to know. We'd only had the one conversation about it, but I didn't want to leave them behind for any reason.

"They're coming with us. Wrath and Shotgun have all the paperwork ready for us. We'll get it on the way out."

"All four of them?" I knew I was grinning from ear to ear.

"Yeah, baby. We've adopted all of them. And you're now Mrs. Aiden Wagner."

"I suppose I should be put out that you didn't get me a wedding ring, but I'm going to trust you to get to the details as quickly as you can." I raised an eyebrow at him.

"You know I will." He chuckled. "Gonna be a handful, woman."

"Like you'd have me any other way. You're president of your MC. How would it look if you had an ol' lady who didn't keep you straight?"

He groaned. "I feel a nightmare coming on. You do that and none of those bastards'll let me live it down."

I stilled then, a thought coming to me. "Is that a bad thing? I was only teasing, Aiden. I won't embarrass you in front of your club. Not ever. At least, not intentionally."

"Honey, there is nothing you could ever say or do that would embarrass me. Why? Because you love me. You'd never do anything maliciously. Good fun is good fun. Besides, anyone who sees us together knows I love you too." He wrapped his arms around me, and I clung to him.

"I never told you I loved you. How'd you know?"

"Like I said. Anyone who sees us together knows. I know."

"And you love me?"

"With all my heart and then some, baby."

I sniffed, trying to blink back tears but failing miserably. "If my life could be any more perfect, I don't know how it could happen. It's all thanks to you, Aiden." I looked up at him. "I do love you. Heart and soul. Thank you for all you've done for me. For all you've given me."

"All I've given you was myself. I'm your man, and I always will be."

"I'm yours too. Forever."

"Yeah, baby. Forever."

Deadeye (Bones MC 13)
A Bones MC Romance
Marteeka Karland

Chloe -- Manipulative on the best of days, my mother hooked up with the president of a powerful MC. When he retired, she decided to give me to a man I've never met. Guess she thought she'd still be able to keep her status if I became the ol' lady of the new president. I have no idea what the men in the club are like and I'm not judging, but they wear the 1% patch and I know enough about MCs to know that can't be good for a girl like me.

Deadeye -- I'm a patient man. Pride myself on that. So when I find a girl camping out under a rock watching the club, I camp out to watch her. The more I watch, the more I like what I see. Before I can make her mine, though, I need to find out why she's here. No one's more surprised than me when she tells me who her daddy is. Except maybe her daddy. Now I'm pitted against one of my own brothers. But the more I get to know the spunky little minx, the more I want her. And the more I realize I may have kill my own MC brother and tear apart a rival MC looking for the woman meant to be their new president's ol' lady.

Chapter One
Chloe

I was tired. So fucking tired. I'd only been on the run for five days, but it was five days of backwoods hell. Finding the place I needed to get to had been hard enough. Actually getting there without anyone seeing me had been a feat like I'd never undertaken before. Still don't know how I managed it without getting hopelessly lost. But here I was.

The name of the club was Bones MC, Somerset, Kentucky. I'd walked all the way from Jeffersonville, Indiana to find this place. Compared to the club I'd come from this one was relatively small. But from what I'd learned, they were very close-knit and incredibly dangerous.

I was currently hiding under a rock overhang just tall enough for me to lie flat on my belly and watch the place. I'd covered myself with leaves and sticks, camouflaging my hiding spot as best I could. So far, no one had spotted me. If they had, they hadn't busted me yet. I should have just gone into the clubhouse, but I wanted to scout the place out first. If there seemed to be too much shady shit going down, I'd just move on without wasting my time. Or putting myself in a worse position than I'd been in when I ran.

So far, there had been parties that got pretty loud and wild, similar to what I'd seen at Iron Tzars MC. The guys at Bones partied hard, but they worked hard, too. Beyond the large clubhouse was a neighborhood. There were what looked like high-end, double-wide mobile homes, but also a smattering of houses, with more going up. The two days I'd been hiding out, I'd seen several of the club members working throughout the day. If there were drug deals or arms sales going down, it wasn't anywhere near their compound. There were women all over the place, but none of them seemed to be there against their will.

The weather was turning. Autumn rain was coming, if the sky was any indication. It was cold and damp, and I had no desire to spend another night under a rock. If I'd judged this place wrong, I was in trouble. Of course, if I didn't get some decent shelter soon, I'd still be in trouble. I'd heard good things about this club in the community. They might not be law-abiding citizens, but they weren't so bad they were feared by the whole city. I was counting on the reputation they'd apparently worked hard to build. If Bones turned out to be a wolf in sheep's clothing, I was fucked, because I had nowhere else to go. And the one man I needed to see here, the one man who could help me in a way I could live with, had no idea I even existed.

Knowing there was nothing else I could find out without getting inside the place, I decided to quit being a pussy and stop stalling. I stood, looking down at my clothes. Having been outside under a rock for the better part of two days, I was filthy. Probably stank too. There was a creek just below my hiding place on the other side of the hill between me and the compound. I could wash there and change my clothes before trying to get inside. If I was lucky, they'd stop me at the gate and take me straight to the man I needed to see. I could only hope he remembered my mother. If not, I was probably screwed.

The wind had started to pick up, and there was a cold bite to it. I knew I needed to hurry, but not bathing and changing clothes simply wasn't an option. If I came to their doorstep looking like a hobo, I was afraid no one would take me seriously. Or, worse, tell me to get the fuck on before they got rid of me.

I stripped, tossing my filthy, damp clothing to the ground. I kept the long-sleeved T-shirt to use as a washcloth, so I didn't have to actually get in the creek. While it was still warm most days, the nights in this part of Kentucky were chilly this time of year. Shallow water, like the lazy stream here, had started to cool, making this bath seriously uncomfortable.

I'd never done this before. Bathed out in the open. In fact, though I'd lived in an MC for most of my life, roughing it wasn't exactly in my repertoire. I'd never been camping. Or hunting. I'd been fishing occasionally but usually on a boat or a dock at the lake. All I'd had to eat the last five days were some snacks I'd managed to sneak out and a couple bottles of water I refilled every chance I got. Now, I was cold, dirty, hungry, and so fucking tired I just wanted to sleep for a fucking week.

"Well, now. What do we have here?" The lazy drawl made me jump and cry out. I tripped and landed on my ass, my naked body on full display. The guy smirked as he looked down at me, his big arms crossed over a powerful-looking chest. His shoulders were wide, stretching the fabric of his Henley, as did his biceps. He had a full beard reaching about halfway down his chest. Cold, assessing blue eyes were fixed squarely on me.

I needed to warn him off. To keep him away from me. But my stupid mouth didn't seem to want to work. I knew from experience bikers responded to strength. I was currently being judged. And probably found sorely lacking.

Finally, I found my backbone. I scrambled to my feet, lifting my chin, making no move to cover myself. That would be seen as a sign of weakness after my hesitation, and I could show exactly none. I made what I hoped was a strong stance, trying to look as unsexy as I could while standing naked. Arms down to my sides, feet slightly apart, I met his gaze with a stern one of my own. "I'm looking for Sword. Lars Gray. I was told he was a member of Bones MC."

The man nodded slowly, still giving me that assessing look. "He is."

"Take me to him."

The guy grinned broadly. "Might want to put some clothes on, little lady. Any woman parading around naked in this club might find herself bent over a pool table."

"I was in the process before you snuck up on me," I snapped. I was more afraid than put out, but I had to make sure I had a good front. I tried to think about how my mom acted in the club. She was the former Prez's ol' lady, and she didn't take shit from anyone. I was so far from her status it wasn't funny, but I had to act like the Prez's daughter if I wanted to reach my goal. "Now, as much as I'm sure you're enjoying the view, I'm going to have to demand you turn around."

He raised his hands. "All right, all right. But you *are* in our territory. Spyin' on our compound."

"I never said I was spying."

"Honey, I've been watchin' you for two days. Only came to get you now because the weather's turnin'. Storm's comin' in tonight, and the temperature's gonna drop. You can't stay out here without protection." He shrugged. "Be easier on everyone to just bring you in."

"Well. Since that was my goal to begin with, more the better. Now. Fucking turn around." I bit out the last between clenched teeth. The big bastard just chuckled but complied.

Quickly, I dressed. I wasn't truly clean, but my clothes were, and I'd gotten most of the dirt off. My hair was the only thing I hadn't been able to give a cursory wash. No help for it now. I'd just have to wait until I found Sword. Hopefully, he'd let me have a place to clean up.

Once I was dressed, the guy gestured for me to walk with him. "Name's Deadeye," he said. "My sniper team gave me that name because I never miss what I'm aiming at. *Ever*. If you're thinkin' of runnin', don't."

"Bones's hospitality leaves a lot to be desired," I muttered. "You threaten all your guests?" I was starting to regret this. I might have jumped from the frying pan into the fire.

"Not when guests use the front fuckin' door, little miss. This is what sneakin' around gets you." He'd seemed like he had a sense of humor before. I was starting to realize that might have been more sarcasm than humor. When I looked up at the guy, there was deadly intent in his gaze. If I ran, I had no doubt he'd come after me.

It wasn't far to the front gate of the compound. Deadeye escorted me inside and straight to the clubhouse. As expected, the noise was deafening. Club girls were interspersed throughout the room, most of them naked. Several of the patched members were there with their women. If they were ol' ladies or steady lays, I had no idea. But they seemed to congregate together away from the club girls and the brothers they were servicing.

"Sword!" Deadeye called the man's name from across the room. I scanned the sea of fucking huge men until I saw one look up at Deadeye. His gaze went from Deadeye to me, then back to Deadeye. The look on his face was bewilderment... then slowly morphed into *rage*.

Sword stood up so fast he knocked his chair over. A woman beside him cried out softly, reaching for him, but he shrugged her off. Then he stomped toward us, his stride getting quicker with each step. The second he was close enough, his hand shot out, and he grabbed me by the throat, squeezing hard. The strength in his grip told me he could break my neck or choke me to death with little effort. It took every ounce of courage and presence of mind I had to stand there passively and not grip his wrist. Doing so would only show weakness. I stood there with my eyes fastened to his and didn't resist at all. The muscles in his forearms bulged, the veins standing out in stark relief. As for his eyes... This man. Was. *Furious*.

"What the fuck, Sword?" I thought that was Deadeye but wasn't sure. My focus was on Sword. Several other men gathered around Sword, seeming unsure what to do. More than one laid a hand on Sword, trying to get him to back off. I could hear voices all around me raised in anger, but they were dim with the increasing roaring in my ears. All I could focus on was the livid features of the man who literally held my life in his hands.

"I don't know what the fuck Bev's playing at, but you tell that Goddamned bitch the next person she sends here leaves in a fuckin' body bag." His voice was deceptively soft but hard as he got in my face, nose to nose. Deadly. Yeah. I was in trouble.

"Sword." The woman from the table was at his side now, one hand on his arm, the other on his shoulder. "Let her go."

"Why are you here, girl?" Sword demanded,

ignoring the woman at his side. "What do you want?"

"Sword!" Another man approached, a woman in tow. When my gaze shifted to them, Sword gripped my neck harder, shaking me slightly.

"Look at me, bitch! Not him!"

"Goddammit, Sword! Fuckin' let her go!"

Sword held my gaze -- and my neck -- for several more seconds. He squeezed just that little bit more. It was enough to cut off my air entirely. It felt like my eyes were bulging out of my head, and my lungs burned. I just held his gaze passively. When he finally let me go, he gave me a hard shove. I stumbled back, tripping as I did. I'd have hit the floor except strong arms closed around me, steadying me on my feet.

I struggled, throwing a high elbow, trying to catch the guy in the chin. "Hey! Take it easy, girl," Deadeye growled at my ear. "It's over. He ain't doin' nothin' else."

"She ain't gone in the next thirty seconds, we'll see what else I ain't doin'." Sword's gaze never wandered from mine. Not to Deadeye, not to the other man, not to his woman.

"What the fuck's goin' on? Deadeye?"

"Been watching her for a couple days, Cain. She's been watchin' the compound. Only called her out cause the weather's turnin'. Storm's comin', and she don't need to be out in it."

"Sword?" Cain turned to him, demanding an answer.

When Sword said nothing, Deadeye continued. "She came here specifically for Sword. By name. And I don't mean his road name, though she knew that as well."

"Sword. Ain't askin' again." Cain sounded nearly as pissed as Sword looked.

"Don't know who she is, but I'd bet my life she's related to Beverly Martin. She and I spent some time together more than twenty years ago. When I first started working for FxFil. Until I figured out she was trying to get information from me."

"Why do you figure she's related to your ex?" Again, Cain's question brooked no argument. Sounded like Sword would answer, or else.

"Because she's a dead fuckin' ringer for Bev! That's why! Could *be* Bev when that woman was younger!"

"Why're you here, girl?" Cain turned his focus on me. My throat hurt where Sword had held his stranglehold on me, but I wasn't about to complain. Or rub my neck.

"Not sure it matters," I muttered. "Seems I made a mistake in coming here. I wasn't expecting a warm welcome, but I'd hoped I could get Sword to listen to me."

"Ain't interested in nothin' you got to say," Sword snapped.

"All right, that's enough." The woman at Sword's side stepped between me and him. "I have no idea what happened in your past with your ex, but I'm betting it was before this girl was even born. Your beef is with Beverly. Not this woman."

"Magenta…"

"I mean it, Sword. I didn't think this was the kind of club who beat up on women for the hell of it! That's where I came from! That's not Bones!"

"Magenta," Cain said softly, though there was a warning in his tone. He didn't sound mean, just… exasperated?

The woman -- Magenta -- ducked her head, turning away. She hurried out of the common room and disappeared through a door in the back.

"Angel, go check on Magenta. Make sure she's good."

"You sure? Seems I might be needed here more." Angel was a beautiful woman in her late thirties or early forties. There were a few threads of gray in her hair and a few laugh lines around her eyes and mouth, but her features spoke of a woman happy with her life. She was slender and barely came up to Cain's shoulder, but then, Cain was tall and broad-shouldered, like most of the men around me. I suddenly found myself wishing she'd stay. If for no other reason than to dilute the abundance of testosterone with a little more estrogen.

"No. I ain't sure. Go on anyway. Magenta needs you. I can fumble my way through this."

"Just don't lose your Goddamned mind like you did with Calliope. You do and you'll be in an even bigger doghouse than Sword. And for a lot longer time." Angel lifted one elegant eyebrow at Cain before glancing over at Sword.

"Fuck!" Sword seemed torn between going after Magenta and finishing the job strangling me. He pointed a finger at me. "State your fuckin' business, then get the fuck out."

"Last I checked, I was president of this fuckin' club," Cain snarled. "Sword, you will stand the fuck down or I'll give you a beatin' like you ain't ever had. *And* strip you of any rank you hold in this club." He turned to me. "What's your name, girl." It wasn't a question, but a demand.

"Chloe," I said, not wanting to give my last name. Not now. It would probably send Sword over the edge. Even though I'd accepted that I'd probably die early in life, I wasn't ready to go at this very moment.

Cain huffed out breath, rapidly losing patience. "Your full name."

"Uh, Cain?" A man came from a room off to the side. He held back an obviously furious woman. She grunted as she struggled to get loose, going so far as to stomp the guy's foot. He winced but held fast. It wasn't a cruel hold, but like he was just trying to keep his woman out of trouble. He was gentle with her even as she fought him.

"Let me go, Data, or I swear I'll sick El Diablo on your ass! Just like I'm getting ready to do to Sword!" She gave Sword a venomous look. I had no idea who or what El Diablo was, but apparently he was bad news.

Sword growled and bared his teeth but said nothing.

"Do not growl at my wife, Sword," Data said softly. There was no "or else." In some ways it was worse than if he'd named the consequence.

"All right, that's enough!" Cain thundered. "You!" He pointed to Data. "Calm your wife down. You!" He pointed to Sword. "Back the fuck off. You're Bohannon's second-in-command but that position can fuckin' change. We don't treat women like you're treatin' this girl unless she's betrayed one of us or the club. If she has, you come to me, and I decide what happens next. And you --" This time he pointed to me. "Start talkin'!"

I lifted my chin. I'd fought so hard to get here. Walked for five fucking days. This was what I wanted, Goddammit! But now, my stubbornness was getting the better of me. It was obvious I'd made some assumptions I shouldn't have.

"Not a good idea to defy Cain when he's in this

kind of mood, girl," Deadeye said at my ear. I jumped, having forgotten he was there. He placed his hand on my shoulder gently as if to calm me. The man was quiet. So still. He had been close to me the whole time and had managed to make himself vanish until he was ready for me to know he was there. "Just tell him what he wants to know."

"Gray," I said with a heated voice. I was a little hoarse and my throat hurt, but I answered Cain's question looking straight into his eyes. "Chloe Gray."

Sword jerked back like I'd struck him, shaking his head. Then he rallied. "No *fucking* way! Lying bitch! No way you're mine! Bev would never allow herself to get pregnant when we were together because she was too focused on her appearance and being the perfect seductress." He practically spat the word seductress. "Besides, I'd have known if she'd gotten pregnant while I was with her."

"She's telling the truth, Sword."

"Zora, no one invited you into this conversation. This is club business." Sword glared at the other woman. She was the one with Data. The woman who looked pissed as hell.

Zora finally broke away from her husband and stomped toward Sword. Without missing a beat, she slapped him. Hard. I half expected the big guy to hit her back, but he just kept his gaze focused on the small woman who now stood shaking her hand. It probably stung worse than Sword's face.

"What the fuck was that for?" Sword actually looked startled. Like he hadn't expected the violence from the woman and had no idea what to do with it.

"For being an insufferable bastard! That woman is *your daughter*, Sword. At least, that's what her birth certificate says. Me and Data started pulling information on her the second Deadeye told us he was bringing her to the compound. If I need to get Mama and Pops in here to do a DNA test, I will. But everything we've pulled on her and her mother points in that direction. Her blood type fits. She was born in an area you were living up until about six months before she was born. And you're right. She's a dead ringer for your ex."

Sword shook his head, then turned back to me. I met his gaze for only the briefest of seconds, just long enough to see the startled look on his face as realization hit him. Then I looked away, feeling tears prick my eyes. No way I'd let this guy see me cry. That was a weakness so profound I'd never come back from it.

"No," he finally said. "It's not possible."

"So you gloved up every time you fucked this girl's mother? Every single time."

"Yeah," Sword said, then darted his gaze away from the other man. "Had one break. Once."

"You stick around long enough to make sure she wasn't pregnant?"

"She was on the pill, for Christ's sake! Sure, I was concerned, but she said she never missed one. It was right before I found out how she'd been playing me. Pumping me for information about ExFil. Bitch was working for the CIA or some shit. Trying to get information about the weapons we get from Argent Tech and the Shadow Demons, and was trying to use me to get it."

"What?" Cain barked his question. "You had a security breach and didn't tell me?"

"No! I'd never put myself in the position of having a security breach! It just took me a while to figure out what she was doin' 'cause I was thinking with my dick and not my brain. But I never broke security protocols, Cain. Never! I never discussed anything with her, and she was never around anything pertaining to our work or any mission. I never kept anything in the house or on my person to do with work. Not even my personal gun. Certainly not anything from Argent. Nothing I had was enough to keep the CIA interested. When I confronted her, she just laughed like it was a big fuckin' joke and I was the butt of it. That was the last day I saw or heard from her."

The president looked hard at Sword, then nodded. "OK. So back to Miss Gray." I really wished he wasn't coming back to me. "Why are you here? No bullshit. Why are you here?"

I put my chin up but felt it trembling. My throat hurt abominably, and I was really on the verge of breaking down. Deadeye's hand on my shoulder tightened fractionally before loosening once more. Encouragement? Or a warning?

"I came here looking for Sword in hopes he'd give me asylum." My voice was getting rougher where my throat was swelling. But if they could ignore what had happened, so could I. I absolutely would not cough or clear my throat.

Sword snorted. "Asylum. You sound just like Bev. Trying to be more sophisticated than you really are. You came from another club. Bitch probably sent you here to spy on us."

I closed my eyes, taking a much-needed calming breath. I was holding on to my temper by a bare thread. "I realize you and my mother had a tumultuous past. She's a manipulative bitch, and I've told her that to her face many times. But you don't know me. I'm willing to bet my mother hurt me a great deal more than she hurt you." The more I spoke the angrier I was getting. Angry and hurt. "I came here hoping one of my DNA donors would give a damn and help me out. I can see now that I was conceived by two equally self-centered assholes." I turned to Cain. "Sir, I'm sorry to have caused such chaos in your club. That wasn't my intention."

"Fuck," Cain muttered as he turned and looked toward the back of the room where Magenta had exited. "Deadeye, bring Chloe to my office. Sword, you get your ass in there too. Data. Zora. I want every scrap of information you've gathered on Chloe in my office in five minutes. Start working on her mother's background. And Sword." He walked to the big man and punched him in the gut. He didn't telegraph the punch, just walked up to the other man and delivered the punishment. Sword grunted and bent double, staggering back a couple steps before bracing himself on a nearby chair. When Sword tried to stand fully upright, Cain snagged his head and yanked sharply down while hiking his knee up so that Sword's face smashed into the president's leg. Cain bent at the waist close to Sword, placing his hands on his knees and speaking very distinctly to his enforcer. "If you treat a woman like you did that girl ever again -- inside this clubhouse or out of it -- I'll cut off your fuckin' balls and apologize to Magenta later."

Sword looked after Cain as the other man straightened, then turned and left the room. Deadeye put an arm around me gently before guiding me after Cain. I stopped in my tracks, suddenly terrified of what was about to happen.

"I know we got off to a rocky start, girl, but I won't let anything happen to you."

"Really? Where were you when Sword was

choking the life out of me?" I turned to glare at him just in time to see him wince. "You told me you were a killer before. I believe you."

"Sword's one of our enforcers. He's the man who's supposed to be preventing shit like he pulled." Deadeye glanced at Sword's retreating form. Sword was following his president as ordered but looked back over his shoulder at us. Was that shame on his face? Regret? "I helped the others try to pull him off you. Wasn't expecting him to do anything like what he did. He's a big bastard, and I was afraid we were going to hurt you in the process."

I shrugged, one tear finally escaping. I was afraid I couldn't stem the flow once they got started, so I wiped this one away with an angry swipe of my hand. "If he's an enforcer in your club, I imagine it's bad form to second-guess his actions with an outsider." With a sigh, I continued on, following the president. "Let's just get this over with. I need to get out of here and keep moving."

"Give us a chance to work this out. Cain's a fair man, and regardless of how we got started with you, Bones does not turn away anyone in trouble. Especially not a woman alone."

"I can take care of myself," I snapped. My anger was making me braver than I really was.

"You look like you walked all the way from Indiana, so I have no doubt you can take care of yourself. But why be on your own when you could have friends helping and looking out for you?"

"Friends. Right." I lifted my chin so he could see my neck. I had no doubt it was red and bruising. "With friends like these…"

Deadeye winced. "Point taken. Just try to open your mind again. You came here for help. Give us one more chance."

When I gave him a slight nod -- after all, I didn't really have any other options -- Deadeye guided me to Cain's office. I honestly didn't think I had one more chance inside me. Not after what Sword had done. I just wanted to avoid another altercation.

Once inside, Cain indicated a leather couch across from his desk. "Have a seat." I sat on one end. Deadeye sat in the middle. Right beside me. So close, his thigh was mashed against mine. He put his arm on the back of the couch behind me, and I found myself wanting him to put it around my shoulders. It was stupid really. He'd been a little crude when he'd found me naked by the stream, but he hadn't touched me. Hadn't said anything overtly harassing. He'd let me dress, then taken me to the clubhouse, expressing concern about me being out in the weather. Of all the men I'd met thus far, Deadeye gave me a calm feeling. Maybe it was the way he could stand perfectly still. I didn't know, but I felt a pull toward him I'd never felt with anyone. My gut was telling me to trust him.

"Now," Cain began as he leaned his forearms on his desk and laced his fingers together. "Tell me what the fuck's going on."

Chapter Two
Deadeye

This girl was cutting out my fucking heart. Her face was heartbreakingly beautiful, her big brown eyes glassy with unshed tears. There were still leaves and twigs in her wildly curling hair, but I'd never seen a more beautiful woman in all my days. The girl was a fighter, too. Strong and stubborn. Sword would probably beat the shit outta me for saying so, but she reminded me a lot of him.

I sent off a hurried text to Goose to have him meet me us outside Cain's office. I was going to need backup for this one, and there was no one I wanted to have my back more than my best and oldest friend.

"My mom was ol' lady to the former president of Iron Tzars MC in Jeffersonville, Indiana. When Warlock decided to retire as president, my mother was furious. Even though the club voted in Warlock's son to replace him, she knew she'd still have some standing in the club, but not like she'd enjoyed as the president's woman. So, she talked Warlock into giving me to his son. I have no idea what she thought to accomplish by doing that. Maybe she thought she'd have some sway over Sting and still have some power if she were his mother-in-law."

"Were you raised in the club?" Cain interrupted.

I shook my head. "No. We came there when I was a teen. Mostly I was away at boarding schools so my mother wouldn't have to deal with me. She only brought me to the club a few times, the last time for Sting to see what she was offering. I took off after that meeting. Not sure how I managed it on foot, but I did. Mom told me about Sword often before she took up with Warlock. She told me he was a bastard, but I didn't want to believe her. I looked him up. Found his service record with a little work. I couldn't believe a Marine who'd served his country so proudly with such distinction could be as horrible as she made him out to be."

She chanced a glance at Sword who sat on the couch, his arms crossed. I knew my brother well enough to know his middle name was now Regret, but he was too stubborn to admit it. Yeah. These two were going to clash continually and spectacularly. I knew I was a bastard for even thinking about it, but I was kind of looking forward to watching the fireworks. Especially after I beat the shit out of Sword so he was careful to never win in those contests of wills.

"So, you were wanting Sword to protect you from being claimed by another club."

"Yes, sir. I can't say they're a bad club, though they wear the one-percent patch. I was only there a couple of times. Warlock was always good to me at home, but he was all about pleasing Beverly. She's a master manipulator. The only thing she wasn't able to get him to do was not retire from being president. They fought over that for weeks before and after he did."

"What about Sting?"

She shook her head. "I only met him once. I'm sure he's as decent as an outlaw biker can be. He wasn't unkind to me during the meeting with Warlock and my mom. Even asked if the union was what I wanted. Mom cut me off before I could answer, but he still asked. I have no wish to be continually pitted between him and my mother."

"So, even knowing your father belonged to an MC, you ran to him for protection." Cain sat back in his chair, his hands steepled. "I take it you're not opposed to living in an MC, then?"

"No, sir. I just want away from my mother. If she keeps trying to mess in the affairs of Iron Tzars, something bad's gonna happen, and I don't want to be caught in the middle. Collateral damage is still hurt. Or dead. And I have no wish to be either."

"So the problem becomes do we keep you here when this other club comes looking for you, or do we turn you over to them."

"I don't want to go with them, but I understand how this puts you in a bad situation." Chloe looked away for a couple of heartbeats before turning back to Cain. "If Sword had known about me, this might have had a different outcome. I guess I built a fantasy around the idea of having a father, so this is on me. I have no idea if Iron Tzars are on my trail, but I stayed off the grid. I took the backroads and wooded areas all the time. I didn't use a debit or credit card, and I don't have a cell phone. I never mentioned wanting to find Sword to my mom, so you guys should be good." She started to get up, but I moved the arm I had over the back of the couch to drape over her shoulders.

"Give us just a few more minutes, girl," I said softly.

"So you propose... what?" Cain continued the conversation seamlessly.

"Nothing. I'll just leave, and if they come knocking at your gates you can tell them whatever you like. I don't want to cause you problems with another club because of my fear and a stupid fantasy, so I won't stay and make life difficult for you when you were just minding your own business." She glanced at Sword briefly. "Or make a fool of myself any longer."

Surprisingly, Sword said nothing. He just watched Chloe interact with Cain. I made a mental note to kick the man's ass double hard when this was done, for not coming to his daughter's aid. His wife would just have to get over it, though I suspected Sword was in the doghouse over this one.

Cain scrubbed a hand over his face. "Fuck." He turned his head and looked out the window for a long moment. Finally, he seemed to make a decision.

"No. You're staying with us. We'll look into the Iron Tzars and see what we're up against, then go from there."

"I'll keep her under my protection," I said.

Cain's gaze snapped to mine. "You sure about this?"

I shrugged. "Wouldn't take the responsibility if I wasn't."

Again, Cain brought his focus back to Chloe. "Do you understand what Deadeye is offering?"

"Enough to know it wasn't exactly an offer," she muttered. When Cain continued to stare at her she took a breath and sighed. "Yes. I understand. Anything I do he can't contain or stop he'll be held accountable for. I'm not here to make trouble, and I'm not a stupid spy. I'm just trying to get away from a bad situation not of my own making."

"All right, then." Cain nodded his head once, then stood. "I'll leave you in Deadeye's capable hands. Angel will look in on you shortly. Make a list of anything you need, and she'll see you have it. That will include a phone. I understand why you don't have one on you, which I think was a good call on your part. But you still need one. Now that you're in our compound, I'll expect you to keep it with you for safety reasons. You need anything for any reason, no matter how trivial, I expect you to get ahold of Deadeye if he's not with you. You can't get him, you'll call Angel or me. Understood?"

She had a bewildered look on her face. I wanted to kiss it off her. "Not really, but I'll do what you say."

"Good. Deadeye, she's all yours." Yeah. If only.

I stood, gently urging Chloe to her feet. "Come on, honey. Let's get you settled."

I thought about getting her a room on the same floor as mine. I hadn't yet taken a house for myself. Attached brothers and their women got first dibs on houses. Besides, I liked being in the clubhouse. I had a room on the top floor where I could see the entire compound. It gave me peace of mind that I was looking over everyone. If there was danger, I'd see it coming. Instead, I just took her to my room.

"I know it's not ideal," I told her when I opened the door and ushered her inside, "but you'll be with me. I'm hoping I can help you feel more secure."

"Uh-huh. You'll also be able to prevent me from leaving."

Girl was smart. "True. But you know you can't do this on your own. You came here for help for that very reason. It's not exactly what you expected, but we're still here to help you. You're getting what you wanted to begin with. No reason to run."

For long moments, we just stared at each other. I wanted her to see I meant what I said about the club wanting to help her, but I also wanted her to know I'd protect her.

"Why?" she demanded. "When you first found me you knew I was watching your compound. Yet you don't believe I'm a spy." Then she tilted her head as if just puzzling out the problem. "Or did you keep me here with you because you *do* think I'm a spy?"

"No, honey," I said. The endearment seemed to be coming off my tongue easily. As if it were the most natural thing in the world. "I don't think you're a spy. I believe you're exactly what you said you were. A woman lookin' for help from circumstances beyond her control."

She nodded, then ducked her head. "I don't know if Sting even wanted me."

Carefully, not wanting to startle her, I stepped closer. Into her private space. I tucked one pale lock behind her ear away from her face. "Honey, there's not a man alive who wouldn't want you."

Her head snapped up, and her gaze locked with mine. "What?" Her voice was a mere thread of sound.

"You heard me. You're a beautiful woman. Brave, too. Not many men I know would have stood their ground like you did when I found you. You entered our clubhouse like a fuckin' princess. To say nothin' of the way you stood your ground against Sword. I've seen seasoned warriors piss themselves when he turns that kind of anger on them. You were fierce as any ol' lady. Any biker who claims not to want you for himself is a Goddamned liar."

She sucked in a breath, her eyes widening. Yeah. There was no way I couldn't kiss her.

Carefully, making sure she had a chance to pull back if she didn't want my touch, I lowered my head to hers. The animalistic part of me was screaming for me to cage her in. To wrap her up in my arms so she couldn't get away from me, but the logical part of my brain knew that would be the worst mistake. Chloe was already skittish. The last thing she needed was to feel like she was being pressured into something she didn't want.

The second my lips made contact with hers, I knew I was in deep trouble. She gasped, her hands going to my shirt. Instead of pushing me away, her hands bunched in the material, and she clutched me to her. She didn't really participate in the kiss. Instead, she just tilted her head up, allowing it as if making up her mind what to do next. Then her fingers relaxed their hold on my shirt, and her hands slid up my chest and shoulders to circle my neck loosely and she fucking sighed. That was my permission.

I grunted my approval before deepening the kiss, my tongue sweeping the seam of her lips, seeking entry. I slid one of my hands to her shoulder while I tunneled my fingers through her hair, being careful to only cradle her head, not to grip her hair.

Then the best sound I'd ever heard filled my ears. Chloe moaned as she settled in and just let me have her. Her tongue gave a tentative stroke against mine, and she shivered. Hell, I wasn't sure *I* didn't shiver. Chloe's kisses were the sweetest I'd ever tasted. As she leaned against me, her body molded itself against me like she fucking belonged there. Maybe she did. I sure as hell wanted her there.

After several seconds, I ended the kiss, not wanting to take things further than she was ready to go. Her eyes were closed, her face tipped up to mine. When she opened her eyes, their pale blue depths seemed to sparkle at me, desire shining when I knew she had no concept of the depths of lust I'd take her to.

I put my forehead against hers as we both struggled to catch our breath. "Fuck me," I muttered. "Never tasted anything so Goddamned sweet."

"I've never been kissed like that." She sounded adorably bemused, like she couldn't quite figure out what had just happened.

"Not sure I have either, baby."

She blinked several times, then stepped back, her eyes going wide and her hand going over her mouth. "Oh, God. I bet I stink."

I shook my head. "No way, honey. You smell like the outdoors. Rich soil. Pine. Foliage. Autumn rain." I grabbed a handful of those pale locks and brought them to my nose. "Mountain breeze... No, baby. You don't stink. At fucking all." Her little whimper was the only thing that helped me regain my control. "Go on. Shower's stocked. Ain't got no girly shit in there, but there's soap and shampoo. Got a couple new toothbrushes still in the pack if you need 'em. Razor, too. Help yourself. I'll be back for you in a couple hours. Get some rest if you need it." I pulled her into my arms once more. "Data says there's a late summer storm comin'. Need to help the brothers make sure everything's closed up and locked down. Feel free to explore the compound if you want to. No one will let you go any place you ain't supposed to be, but they'll guide you gently. If you want to wait, I'll take you around when I get back and we'll explore together. Up to you." She nodded but didn't move toward the bathroom. Instead, she just looked up at me, that adorable, confused look on her face. I leaned in and kissed her gently once more. "Go on now. You'll feel better once you let some hot water relax your muscles."

With another little nod, she finally did as I told her and headed for the bathroom. As I watched her go, I couldn't help but feel like she was just as confused as I was about our attraction. Because there was no doubt she felt it too. I also knew she was my future. I probably didn't deserve her, and I knew she could do better, but it didn't matter. I was keeping her.

* * *

Chloe

What just happened? Had Deadeye actually

kissed me? More importantly, had I actually... *freaking loved it*? I had never even imagined a kiss could be that good. That all-consuming. If he'd backed me to the bed, I'd have gone willingly. I'd have taken everything he had to give and rode out the pleasure to the end and never looked back.

I shut and locked the door to the surprisingly spacious bathroom. There wasn't a tub, but the shower was huge. Just like he'd promised, there was soap and shampoo. No conditioner, but I'd make do without it. I was just grateful for the shower. It was the first real scrub I'd had in weeks. My hair more than anything was really enjoying the cleaning. It had become a tangled mess. I'd just braided it as tightly as I could to keep it from turning into a complete rat's nest.

Stepping out, I reached for a towel and dried myself. I'd lost weight during my long-ass hike. I could see my ribs as I glanced at myself in the mirror. I tried to ignore it, but it was no use. I knew my clothes fit looser, but this was ridiculous. Also, my neck was now sporting dark red bruises, thanks to my asshole father. I'd have to be careful. Really feel these guys out. If there were more here who had Sword's temperament, I could be in worse trouble than I'd been in before.

Though my hair now felt like heaven, by far the best thing in that bathroom was the toothbrush and toothpaste. That was the bomb! Of course, then I realized I'd probably tasted awful to Deadeye. I mean, I'd brushed my teeth, courtesy of the little disposable toothbrushes I'd had in my pocket. I'd kept them until there wasn't much left, the five-pack lasting well beyond what they should have. But I'd still brushed my teeth. Just sans toothpaste. I groaned. My humiliation was now complete.

When I stepped out of the bathroom, there was a

change of clothes on the bed. Underwear still in the pack, a soft pair of jeans, and a T-shirt. I had no shoes, but really, I didn't need them inside the compound. I'd thought I'd do like Deadeye suggested and take a nap before he returned, but my curiosity got the better of me. It was my fatal flaw. It was that same curiosity that had me listening to my mother and father argue over giving me to Sting. They hadn't told me the reason for the visit to the Iron Tzars clubhouse, but once inside, after I'd met Sting, I'd lost myself in the throng of people and snuck out.

The way I saw it, that arrangement was a no-win situation for me. If Sting accepted me, I'd continually be put between my mother and my husband. That could land me in big trouble with the club. Sting as well. Which meant he'd have to take care of me. I doubt bikers like him did it with a simple spanking. Or even a beating. He'd disappear me where no one would ever find my body. On the other hand, if he rejected me, I'd be humiliated. It could even trigger the rest of the club to take their fill of me. At least, that's what I'd heard could happen. Either way, I'd split. And ended up here. Might as well take a look at my surroundings in case I needed to make a quick getaway.

I left the room, walking down the hallway to the stairs. The building was laid out in a square with rooms on either side of the hallway, the hall coming around the perimeter to meet itself. It was more like a hotel than an MC clubhouse.

When I rounded the corner, I nearly tripped over Sword. He was seated with his back to a closed door, his knees bent and his forearms resting on them. As I scrambled back, he looked up at me and winced.

"Hey, girl."

"My name's Chloe." The very last thing I wanted to do was confront Sword. He didn't want me around, and I could now say the feeling was definitely mutual. The man was a serious ass. I eyed him warily.

"Yeah." He winced, scrubbing a hand over his face. "I'm sorry. Chloe."

I started back down the hall and go to the stairs from another direction, but he called out to me. "Maybe we started this all wrong, Chloe."

"No shit," I muttered.

"Can we start over?"

I shook my head. "Not interested."

"Come on, girl -- er, Chloe." He stood, looking contrite and like it actually mattered to him if I rejected him or not, and held out a hand to me. Like he fully expected me to take his freaking hand! "I'm sorry. I overreacted."

"You think?" I took another step back, putting a hand out defensively. "Stay back, Sword."

"I ain't gonna hurt you."

I tilted my head so there was no way he could fail to see the reddish-blue bruising he'd put on my neck. "All evidence to the contrary."

Sword turned his head away, shaking it slightly as he winced. "I'll never forgive myself for that." His voice was low and husky. "I'm sorry, Chloe. You didn't deserve my anger."

I shrugged. "Apology accepted. Now. If you'll excuse me." I started back down the hall, trying to be flippant about the whole thing when I was really starting to tremble in fright. He might be sorry now, but I was betting it was more for whatever reason he was sitting outside in the hallway than because of what he'd done to me. The last thing I wanted to happen was for him to see how badly he frightened me.

"Chloe, please." Sword kept trying to engage me when all I wanted to do was get the hell out of there.

"It was a stupid idea for me to go roaming around without Deadeye," I muttered.

"*No.*" Sword's voice was firm. Adamant. "I know I didn't exactly give you the impression you were safe here, and you have every right to hate me. But don't let my actions color your view of Bones. We're not bad people. No one here would ever hurt you. *I* should never have hurt you, and I'll pay for it later. I deserve everything I've got coming."

I wanted to confront him. Wanted to tell him that, yes, he damned well deserved whatever punishment he was expecting. But I just wanted to get back to the relative safety of the Deadeye's room.

"It's fine. Really." I waved him off. "But I'm tired. Deadeye suggested I take a nap. I should have done that instead of venturing out on my own."

"At least let me walk you back." Sword looked really upset. Like he knew he'd fucked up and had no idea how to make it right. Well, he'd be right. I didn't know how he could make it right either.

I shrugged. "It's a free country. Can't stop you from walking."

Thankfully, it wasn't very far to Deadeye's room. I reached for the door, but Sword got there first. He opened the door, then stepped back to allow me to enter. "If you need anything, I'll be out here." He hiked a thumb, pointing down the hall. "Makin' sure the club girls leave you alone."

I didn't acknowledge him. I just wanted to be away from him. Shutting the door, I turned and put my back against it, sliding down the wood to sit on the floor. Now that there was a safe barrier between us, I trembled, my breath coming in little pants. I'd tried to put up a good face, but the man scared the bejesus out of me. And this man was supposed to be my father? I had no idea what I'd walked into, but I had a feeling I'd better be figuring out a way to leave. Sooner rather than later.

Chapter Three
Deadeye

"Gonna be a bad one," Data said as he toggled from one screen to the next. Each held some kind of weather radar from different sources. "Definitely severe thunderstorms if not tornadoes. Not exactly the season for it, but the weather's been wonky this year. This is going to be a cross between an ice storm and a severe thunderstorm. Wouldn't surprise me to see a tornado outta this motherfucker, rare as they are." He looked up at Cain. "I'd feel better if everyone spent the next few hours in the basement. Or at least on the ground floor. This storm's got everything. Rain. Snow. Ice. Wind. Even lightning."

"How many people in the compound or on the grounds?" Cain kept his gaze steady on Data as he tried to get all the information he needed before making a decision.

"More than fifty counting club girls. Most of the members are in the clubhouse. The ones with families not living in the main building are in their assigned houses in the neighborhood. They all have basements."

"Good. I want everyone in the clubhouse to go to the basement. No exceptions. It'll be crowded, but there should be enough room. How much time before it starts?"

Data shrugged. "Give or take an hour."

"Good. Anyone who doesn't want to follow orders needs to leave the grounds now and get to whatever shelter they want. Members staying in their houses need to make sure their families head to the basement until the storm's passed."

"Looking like, once it hits, it'll stick around for several hours. Maybe until morning. Big-ass system,

Cain."

"Until morning, then. Get it done."

Data sent out a mass text alert. Soon, cell phones began to beep and buzz all over the common room. I headed up the stairs to my room to collect Chloe. Goose had been shadowing me since I got to Data's command center, staying out of sight, but I knew the man was there. He'd watch our backs until I gave him the all clear. I'd put him on Chloe when I wasn't with her. Anything seemed out of place, he'd take care of it. This wasn't how I wanted to spend my first night with her, but I wanted her safe. If that meant huddling with her in the basement surrounded by my brothers, I'd see what I could do to make that time more interesting.

When I got upstairs, I found Sword sitting outside my door looking as miserable as anyone could look. Didn't mean I was gonna be civil to the motherfucker.

"What the fuck are you doing here, Sword?" I stomped toward the older man, looking as intimidating as I could. Given Sword was the enforcer of Bones and backup Sergeant at Arms should Bohannon be out of commission, I knew he wouldn't intimidate easily. Sure enough, the big fucker just scowled at me.

"Last time I checked I was an officer in this club, and you're just a wet behind the ears fucking prospect."

"I've been a member for years! What the fuck?"

"Know that can change if you fuck my daughter."

I'd never wanted to throat-punch someone more than I did Sword in that moment. "Why? I mean, pleasurin' such a beautiful woman can't possibly compare to nearly stranglin' the life out of her." I jabbed a finger at him. "You lost the right to forbid me anything regarding Chloe the moment you laid hands on her, you son of a bitch. You were nothing but hostile toward her. And if she agrees to be mine, I'm going to kick your ass on principle. Might any-fuckin'-way." Sword scowled at me, his face growing thunderous. Yeah. I was being disrespectful, but he'd done worse to a woman who'd sought him out specifically for help. A woman who we were certain was his flesh-and-blood daughter. "You don't like my attitude? Take it to Church. Let every motherfucker in this place vote on which one of us was in the wrong. They agree it's me? I'll take Chloe and leave. You may not be interested in protectin' her, but I sure as fuck am."

"You don't get to lecture me, boy. If my daughter decides you're the man for her, we'll mix it up outside. Until then, watch your fuckin' mouth or I *will* have a go at you. You won't like the outcome."

"Why are you outside my fuckin' room?"

He shrugged. "Chloe ran into me on her way downstairs. Backtracked to her room almost as soon as she saw me. Which was when I realized you really had put her in *your* room." He glanced off. "She's afraid of me, and by extension, the club. She's a runner. Just wanted to make sure she didn't leave. You know. With the storm comin' and all."

"Uh-huh. And why do you suppose she's afraid of you, huh?" He just glared at me. "Well, I'm here now. I'll watch over her until we can get this all sorted out." I squatted down so I was at eye level with him. "And if you say one more fuckin' word to her I don't much like, I'll figure out a way to kill you. Cain, Torpedo, and Bohannon will just have to get over it."

I opened the door to my room and stepped

inside, intending to close the door behind me. Instead, Sword's foot blocked me. I wanted to punch a motherfucker.

"I wanna talk to her." He stuck his chin up, demanding I comply.

"I'll relay the fuckin' message, Sword. Now get the fuck out."

Before I could get the door shut, a cool breeze hit my face that shouldn't be there. I frowned, forgetting about locking Sword out. I turned and marched across the room... where the window was wide fucking open, the sheers blowing in the cool autumn air.

I looked out the window. Sure enough, the escape ladder I had installed on the side of the building next to my window was lowered. There was no sign of Chloe, but there was no doubt she'd run.

"Motherfuck!" I pulled out my phone, sending a text off to Goose. I thought for a moment and included Cliff, too. I knew he was standing guard at the gate.

"She ran. Didn't she." Sword wasn't asking a question.

I turned to face the other man. "When I find her, if I can coax her back, I'm giving you a beatin' like you ain't ever even conceived of."

"Fine," he said. "But I'm going with you to find her."

I gave Sword a crisp nod, knowing my brother would be the best asset I could have. Besides, no matter their differences, no matter how horribly Sword had treated Chloe, I knew he regretted it. I'd never keep him out of a hunt this important. Even if I actually had the authority.

We headed out the window the way Chloe had gone. Once me and Goose found her trail, we'd find her. I wasn't worried she'd disappear on me as much as I was worried about the approaching storm. The temperature had already fallen with the darkness. The wind was picking up, and there was a decided bite to it. Any rain would be bone-chilling and could quite possibly be ice. If it got as bad as Data thought it might, the wind as well as lightning would pummel the area. Finding Chloe before it hit in full force was imperative. Her very life could depend on it.

* * *

Chloe

The wind was blowing through colder than I'd expected. I'd snagged a coat from Deadeye's closet figuring he'd get over it, but I didn't have gloves or any kind of garment to shed water. It had started to rain in great, freezing sheets. The temperature had dropped, and ice was starting to form on the trees and grass. Finding adequate shelter was even harder than it had been when I was staking out the Bones compound.

I'd run as far as I could before the storm hit, moving for an hour and a half before the wind and rain forced me to stop. I'd managed to find a grouping of low-hanging trees where I huddled in a small depression. It did nothing to stop the freezing rain, and soon I realized I was in big trouble. Not only was the rain picking up and the icy wind chilling me to the bone, but lightning streaked the sky followed by booming thunder. There was no way I could stay under the trees. I needed real cover. Since I was deep in the woods, there was none.

I'd seriously fucked up. I was convinced I needed to leave the club because of the reception I'd received from Sword, but honestly, why did I expect anything different? He'd had no idea I existed. Obviously, my mom had done a number on him in some way. Her talent was to manipulate people.

No. That wasn't my fault. I might look like my mother when she was younger, but Sword had to know I wasn't her. I hadn't done anything to him to deserve the wrath he'd given me. And yeah. I was terrified of the man.

Knowing I needed to get moving, I pulled Deadeye's big coat around me as much as I could and moved from the trees just as another booming round of thunder sounded in the distance. I was soaked to the skin and freezing cold. Lightning flashed followed by a closer thunderclap. I didn't have any kind of GPS or even a fucking map, but I had the lay of the land firmly in my mind from my trek here. I knew I was headed toward a road leading out of the woods and into a more populated area. I just wasn't sure exactly how far it was.

Stumbling around in the dimming light, I fell more than once. The cold was growing unbearable now, my muscles stiffening, making it hard to keep my balance. The ice and cold -- and my tears -- stung my eyes.

I sobbed out a miserable, terrified cry, the sound torn from me as I looked around trying to get my bearings. Which was when I realized I was completely and utterly lost.

A bright flash of lightning blinded me, followed by a sharp crack and a deafening boom of thunder. My insides vibrated with the noise as I covered my ears with a scream. Then something hit my shoulder and I spun around, looking around for whatever had hit me. I spied a small limb from one of the trees and looked up...

Just in time to see another huge limb crashing down on me. I tried to dive out of the way, but there was no way to move that fast, especially not in my present condition. All I managed to do was fall and turn to my back as the limb landed with a *thud* and a rustle of leaves. My legs were pinned beneath the heavy wood. Surprisingly, the pain wasn't as bad as it should have been. Looking around, I saw the branch had fallen at an angle so the full weight hadn't hit me, but it was heavy enough I couldn't pull myself free, and I thought my ankle was stuck between two rocks or something. There was no way I could push the heavy thing off me either. I was trapped. And fucking terrified!

"Help!" I have no idea why I was screaming for someone. It wasn't like anyone knew where I was. Even if they did, there was no way they could hear me over the roaring wind, thunder, and pounding rain. I tried with all my might to move, to free myself. I was so cold my muscles didn't want to work, and the wind was making it so much worse.

I sobbed openly now. This was how I died. My own stupidity was going to kill me.

All I could do was wrap Deadeye's coat around me as tight as I could. It was soaked, but there was still a hint of his masculine scent. I clung to that when I had no reason to. He'd never come after me. Even if he did, he'd have no hope of finding me. I had no idea even how far away I was from the compound. The one thing I absolutely did not want to acknowledge was that he might not give a damn. Why would he? I was a complication his club didn't need. I also wasn't accepted by Sword, the only tie I had to the club. So, why would they even consider letting me stay, let alone coming after me when I ran? Especially in this weather.

I closed my eyes. I still shivered, but I didn't feel

as cold as before. Maybe the temperature was rising a little? I looked up into the driving rain that pelted down on my face. Other than being cold, it was peaceful out here. I mean, the thunder was loud and the lightning abrupt, but there was no one telling me what I had to do with my life. No one telling me I had to marry someone I didn't know and was more than a little afraid of. No one telling me I wasn't good enough or smart enough or pretty enough. No one was telling me they didn't want me.

The earth wanted me. Nature. It had made that abundantly clear by dropping a tree limb on me. If I was going to die, at least I was with someone who wanted me.

* * *

Deadeye

When the weather turned, it turned in a fucking hurry. Data had been right. This was as bad a storm in autumn as I'd ever seen. I wasn't too worried, though. I'd found her tracks, and Sword and I had hit the woods, Goose right with us but shadowing us from a distance. He would be looking out for anything we missed in our hurry. Since Sword was with me, that left Bohannon on Cain. As president of Bones, he wasn't left unguarded when there was a questionable threat. Given the fact Chloe had run *and* the possibility of another club coming to our door, no one was taking chances with Cain.

I didn't become too alarmed until the rain started to come down in sheets, the lightning illuminating the sky in angry flashes. Then the temperature dropped even more, and the rain started to freeze anything it touched. It didn't take fifteen minutes for everything to be covered in a thin layer. And it was absolutely *pouring.*

"Call back to the clubhouse," I yelled to Sword. "Have someone bring a couple of side-by-sides. We're gonna need 'em before we get done."

Sword nodded his agreement and took out his phone, texting furiously.

We kept moving deeper into the woods. With each passing minute I grew more and more alarmed. There was ice everywhere. I had no idea what Chloe was wearing, but I'd bet she wasn't dressed for the weather any more than she had been when I'd found her earlier today.

"Chloe!" I yelled her name, hoping like hell she'd hear me and yell back. It was a futile gesture, because the wind was so fierce it whipped the words straight back into my face. "Chloe!"

I glanced at Sword. He was yelling her name too, but I could barely hear him. There was no way she'd hear us from any distance.

We kept moving. Her trail was faint because of all the weather, but I'd had more experience tracking people than I cared to admit. I wasn't usually so close to my target, but I'd had to track my prey before I set up my nest to watch for the perfect moment for the kill. I was using every bit of my tracking skills now.

The longer I went without spotting her, the more alarmed I became. The storm still raged, the sky illuminating with each streak of lightning, the air booming with the following thunder. With the wind and ice, I knew I could easily pass right by Chloe and never know it if I wasn't careful. I'd lose her trail and might not ever find it again. I glanced to my right and spotted Goose in the darkness and rain. He pointed in the same direction we'd been heading, wanting me to go on.

I tried to go carefully so I didn't miss a sign, but it was hard. I wanted to run until I found her. She had at least an hour's head start on us. I thought she was trying to head toward the main road, but she'd strayed off course and instead headed deeper into the woods. There was a bluff about a mile from here that fell into the lake. That was the only thing of importance in the direction she was headed.

Goose whistled low, motioning for me to come to him. It took little time to see her tracks carried me in that direction. When I came on a little depression at the base of a close group of trees, I paused. It looked like a place she'd try to take shelter, though it was woefully inadequate. It was the only place I'd seen where she could curl up and hunker down. If the wind wasn't constantly shifting directions, the trees would probably keep most of the freezing rain off her. At least, it would have at the beginning. Now, there was no way it sheltered her.

There were more tracks nearby. Like she had stopped here but moved on.

Then I saw it just as Goose pointed.

A large limb had fallen from the tree above. It looked like it had been snapped by the lightning, but it was hard to tell in the dark. I shone my light all around until I saw Chloe. My heart nearly stopped.

She lay still as death. The only evidence she was still alive was the gentle puff of fog from her warm breath. She'd taken my jacket but other than that had no protection from the elements. And she was soaked to the skin.

"Sword! Over here!" I waved my light at him to get his attention. The second I saw his light swing in my direction, I turned my attention back to Chloe.

The limb had fallen on her, but I had no way of

telling how much damage it had done. She was pinned across her thighs. If the branch had crushed her legs, lifting it could let her bleed out. But there wasn't really a choice. We had to get her out of the elements.

I knelt beside her, stroking her wet hair out of her face. "Chloe! Chloe, honey, wake up!" I put every ounce of command I had into my voice. It was the voice I used when giving orders in the field. The voice no one disobeyed.

Her eyes fluttered open, and I thought I might pass out with relief. "Sword! Where are the guys with those side-by-sides? We need them now!"

"They're on their way, but it will take time to get here. And they have only the vague directions I've been giving them. Trees and dropoffs aren't easily maneuvered around."

"I'll go bring them to you." Goose put his hand on my shoulder. "You'll need them to help get the tree off her. She's pinned down."

Sword got to his knees, trying to see the damage done to her legs while I whipped off my coat and covered her with it. "There you go, baby. It's not much, but it's warm and will keep the rain off." I turned back to Goose. "Go. Hurry." With a nod, Goose turned and sprinted away from us.

"What about you?" Chloe's voice was small. Thin. Her eyes seemed to struggle to stay open. "I'm not really that cold anymore."

"I'm fine, baby. But we need to get you out from under this limb. Where do you hurt?"

She shook her head. "Nowhere. Just... sleepy..."

"You stay awake!" I barked my order with every ounce of command in my body. "Under no circumstances will you fall asleep, you hear me?"

"Bossy..."

"Damned straight. And you'll *obey* me." I put emphasis on the word obey in hopes of getting a rise out of her. She desperately needed some adrenaline pumping through her blood. Anything to keep her talking and engaged.

"Obey you? I don't even like you."

"No?"

"No. You're too bossy." She didn't turn her head away from me, her gaze clinging to mine.

"Tell you what, baby." I talked to her as Sword, and I continued to evaluate the situation with the log. It didn't look like it had actually crushed her legs. The limb had caught on something and gave her just enough room not to injure her but had pinned her securely beneath it. "You do what I tell you to until I get you safely back to the clubhouse, then you can boss me around all you want."

She was quiet for a moment. I had to glance back at her to make sure she hadn't closed her eyes. Surprisingly, she looked back at me intently, like she was considering all the embarrassing things she was going to make me do.

"Fine. If you can get me out of here, the least I can do is obey you, I guess."

"That's my girl. Now. If we do anything that hurts, you have to tell us immediately. Understand?"

"We?"

"Yeah. Me and Sword are gonna get you outta here." She whimpered and pulled my coat higher, as if hiding her head would keep Sword from seeing her. "Honey, we just want to help you. I swear, no one's gonna hurt you."

"He will," she whispered. In the howling wind and pouring rain, I nearly missed what she'd said. It made my chest hurt and my jaw clench. I glanced up at

Sword. If I thought Sword regretted his outburst when he'd first seen Chloe, I knew it now. He looked like he'd been gutted. Good enough for the bastard.

"He won't, baby. Because when we get out of here, I'm going to kick his ass. Just for you."

She gave me a fierce look. "Do you promise?"

"With all my heart, baby. I'll make it good too."

"We've got to get her out from under this damned log," Sword bit out. "The others are close, but it's slow going. Road's not far from here. Once they get to us and she's free, it won't take nearly as long to get her back to the compound."

"Can you see what it's caught on? I don't want to risk moving it if there's a chance it could slip and really hurt her."

There was a pause before Sword answered me. "It's a risk no matter what we do. But she needs out of the water and mud or she's gonna freeze. Besides, that brace is shaky at best. One good puff of wind or another branch falls and it'll give." He scrubbed his hand over his face. "Wish Goose had stayed until we got her free."

He was right. It was a risk. "We could wait for the others. Could be half an hour before they get to us with the terrain the way it is. Even with Goose leading them to us." I didn't want to. I wanted Chloe out of her prison and in my arms where I could keep her safe.

"We could…"

Yeah. I got it. He didn't want her under there a second longer than she needed to be.

Sword and I locked gazes for long moments before we came to a silent agreement. We'd be doing this now rather than waiting on help.

"I'll lift this motherfucker." Sword tested the weight and balance of the log, changing positions a few times before satisfied he was going about it the most efficient and safest way. I knew because it was what I'd do. "OK." He steadied his stance. The limb was too low to the ground to lift with his legs or put on his shoulder to let his legs take the brunt of the work. He had to lift with his arms and back, which would not only put a strain on Sword's back but make the lift even more dangerous. If he slipped, Chloe could be in a worse position than she was now. "You ready?"

"Don't you drop it before I tell you, Sword. I can lift it if you can't." Sword was a big-ass, stout motherfucker, but he was also in his mid-fifties. As angry as I was at him, I didn't want him to be seriously hurt.

"Just get her free, you bastard. I won't drop it." I could see by the look in his eyes he was dead serious.

"OK then. On three."

Sword counted it down. The second he lifted, I pulled Chloe, trying to get her free of the downed log. She cried out, and her body refused to move any farther. With the log off the ground, I immediately saw the problem. Her ankle was caught between a rock and an exposed root.

"Fuck!" I swore as I let her go to scramble to her foot and pull at her leg, trying to free her as quickly as I could.

"Hurry!" Sword's voice was strained as he yelled at me.

Try as I might, I couldn't free her ankle. The rock seemed to have some give to it, but not enough for me to pull her free. I was about to tell Sword to lower the limb when I saw another problem. The branch holding it off Chloe's leg had shifted when had Sword lifted the limb pinning Chloe. If he let it go, the heavy branch would crush any part of Chloe's slight body pinned beneath it.

"Fuck!" I started digging with my hands, trying to pry either the rock or the root to move it just that little bit. Sword cried out, pain on his face, but he didn't let go. He bellowed with the strain, still holding the log above Chloe's leg. The second I freed Chloe's ankle, I pulled her legs back and rolled over twice, taking her with me as Sword dropped the log.

"Did you get her?" Sword's voice shook. "Is she hurt?"

"I got her. She's good." I had no idea if she was good, but I knew I'd gotten her free before Sword had dropped the log. "Look at me, Chloe!" She was cradled in my arms. I sat on the ground trying to assess her injuries as much as I could. There was nothing obvious other than probably hypothermia. "Look at me!"

Rain pelted her face, making her eyes squint. Even in the small amount of light from the flashlight in my hand I could see her struggling to keep her eyes open as water streamed down steadily onto her face. Ice formed on the ends of her lashes. I didn't shine the light in her face, even though I needed to see her clearly. That would make her very uncomfortable when she was already freezing and terrified. She managed to look up at me, obeying me like I'd told her to.

"Good girl," I said, smiling as much as I could. It was fucking cold, and I was very afraid for her as wet as she was. "Can you move your feet for me?" She nodded and wiggled both her feet slightly. "How about your legs? Can you bend your knees?" Again, she did as I asked. "Pain?" She shook her head. Sword wasn't hovering over us so I assumed he was trying to keep his distance so Chloe wouldn't freak out.

Faintly, I heard the small engines of the side-by-sides as they made their way to us. The lights weren't far, and I waved my flashlight in the air like a beacon. That was when I noticed Sword wasn't doing the same.

"Sword? You good?"

"Yeah. All good. Is Chloe hurt?"

"Not that I can tell. But I'd bet my ass she's got hypothermia."

"Need to get her warmed up and in dry clothes." Sword sounded strained, but I could only take care of one person at a time. Sword could look after himself a few minutes longer.

"The brothers are almost here. Just hang on a little longer." I wasn't sure if I was talking to Chloe or Sword. I was pretty sure the other man had injured himself, but I had no idea what he'd done.

It wasn't long before the ATVs pulled up beside us. Three men jumped out of one, two the other.

"She good?" That was Scout. He was a new addition to the club, but a man I knew from ExFil. He was solid as a rock under fire and a deadly hunter.

"I think so. Freezing. I'll get her to the vehicle. Go check on Sword. I think he's hurt."

I stood with Chloe's slight weight in my arms. Carrying her to the vehicle, I talked to her as soothingly as I could. She still looked up at me, blinking the icy rain away. Her face was pale, and her lips had a bluish tinge to them. She wasn't shivering.

"We gotta get her to the clubhouse. Fast." Thankfully, the guys had packed several blankets in the back seat of one side-by-side. I set Chloe down and snagged one, wrapping it around her shoulders.

"We need to move quickly." Cliff, Cain's adopted son, snagged another blanket. I assumed it was for Sword. "The temperature's still dropping. The ATV's not fully enclosed, and we gotta move. Wind's gonna be brutal."

I nodded once, taking his meaning. "Go see what's goin' on with Sword. I'll get her out of her wet clothes and call the second we're ready." Cliff nodded, then left us. "I'm sorry, honey. But I've gotta get you out of these wet clothes. You're cold enough as it is. It's gonna get worse when we pull out of here." She just looked up at me, still keeping her eyes on me. I got the feeling I was her anchor, but that might have been wishful thinking.

Chloe didn't stop me when I pulled off her wet shirt and bra, tossing the wet garments into the back of the vehicle. I wrapped the wool blanket around her shoulders before pulling her to her feet to pull her pants down her legs. I sat her back on the seat while I finished, also tossing them to the back. Her shoes and socks followed before I wrapped her head to toe in blankets and pulled her into my lap, calling out to Cliff we were ready.

When he got to the driver's side, Cliff pulled out one last blanket and tucked it around both of us. "Hang on to her. Once we get clear of the woods and on the road, we're gonna fuckin' move."

"Just get us back to the compound. I'll take care of Chloe. Sword OK?"

"Not sure. He can't move his arms. My money's on torn biceps, but that'll be up to Mama to determine."

"He lifted that limb so I could get Chloe out. Had to hold it longer than he should have because her foot was stuck."

"Yeah? Well, he definitely did his part." He glanced at Chloe as he started the ATV. "Hope she appreciates it."

My gaze snapped to Cliff. "She doesn't owe him

anything, Cliff. It's his fault she ran in the first fuckin' place. If he injured himself helpin' her, it's just payback for how he injured her." My tone was harsh. Angry. I didn't want Sword hurt, but Goddamnit, I didn't want anyone judging Chloe for this. If it was anyone's fault, it was mine for leaving her alone too long. I should have known she wouldn't want to stay in the same building with Sword, and I didn't blame her.

"Just making an observation, Deadeye. He's really fuckin' hurt. And he did it for her. He's still asking if she's OK."

"I get it. I'll make sure she knows he saved her."

Cliff sighed but took off through the woods. The way was hard going until we finally made it to the road. Then Cliff hauled ass, pushing the side-by-side as hard as it would go until we reached the compound. And home.

Chapter Four
Chloe

The ride back to the clubhouse was a blur. I didn't want to go but was grateful I wasn't dead, so I didn't protest. Well, that *and* I was chilled to the bone. I was numb with cold and so drained I could barely stay awake. I'd have dozed off if Deadeye hadn't constantly demanded I look up at him or answer some stupid question like what day it was or what my name was. Anything to keep me talking to him when all I wanted to do was sleep.

Somehow, we ended up in a bathroom. There was a female voice giving instructions, but I couldn't make out most of it. I was in some kind of twilight stage between sleep and wakefulness. I knew I was naked and that Deadeye had me in his arms, but I couldn't seem to make myself protest. His body was hot, almost uncomfortably so, but he felt so good against my chilled flesh.

In a way, it was almost worse to be warming up. My skin seemed to prickle with a million needles, the pain going from uncomfortable to nearly unbearable the longer he held me. Also, he took me into the shower with him, sitting on a bench with me in his arms while hot water poured over us in a gentle fall. That was when the pain really set in.

I cried out, begging for him to let me go, needing to get away from the water, but he refused.

"Shh, baby." He nuzzled my hair, kissing my temple. "I know it hurts. You're so cold. We've got to warm you up. The water's not that hot. Just lukewarm."

"Hurts," I managed weakly, whimpering.

"I know. I'm sorry. I know, baby. Gotta get you

warmed up, though. You'll feel better then." He rocked me gently, continuing to murmur softly to me. Through the pins and needles over my skin, I thought he probably wouldn't want anyone to know how he was treating me just now. It certainly didn't fit with the biker persona I'd gotten used to and expected. Warlock might have given my mother anything she wanted, but that was more because he let her manipulate him rather than any tenderness on his part. At least, that was the impression I got.

Gradually, the stinging subsided, and I started shivering. I actually wanted him to make the water warmer, but was too afraid to ask. Fortunately, Deadeye seemed to be very good at reading people. At least, he was good at reading me. He moved slightly, and the water heated up just a little. I moaned, unable to hide my reaction. The heat felt wonderful. It felt like I would never be warm again, but now I was getting there.

"Better, honey?"

"Yeah." Even to my own ears, I sounded drowsy. The sigh was as much contentment as it was exhaustion. "Getting warm."

"Good. We'll just sit here a little while longer. Then I'll have Mama check you over good. She says you're not hurt, we'll go to bed."

"But, Iron Tzars --"

"Can wait until tomorrow. At least for us. Once we found you, Data, Zora, and Suzie turned their complete focus to digging into every single member of Iron Tzars, including Warlock and Sting. We'll know everything there is to know about them by the time you wake up. Now. Just relax and let me take care of you a little while longer. Can you do that?"

I wanted to tell him I could take care of myself,

but my abilities in that department were really being called into question. Besides, it felt nice in his arms. For such a gruff man when I first met him, Deadeye was being incredibly gentle with me now.

I took in a breath before letting it out in a little resigned sigh. "Are you angry with me?"

He stiffened. "What? Why would you think I was angry? Have I scared you, honey?"

"No. It's just... You had to come after me in an ice storm."

"Oh, it was more than just ice. There was wind and lightning and really, *really* cold rain. And ice." I couldn't tell if his tone was teasing or chastising. My mind was still sluggish, and it was all just too much to process.

I winced, turning my head into his chest. If he was going to put me down, I wanted every possible second in his arms. Because, by God, it felt fucking *good*. "I'm so sorry."

"You got nothin' to be sorry 'bout. You're scared. I get it. Could your timing have been better? Hell, yeah. But I don't in any way blame you for this."

I decided not to examine his words too closely. I needed sleep before trying to figure everything out.

It wasn't long before Deadeye turned off the shower and carried me out, sitting me on the vanity. He wrapped a towel securely around me before taking a brush out of the pack and working with my hair.

"You'll need to wash it later, but once Mama looks you over, I'll help you dry it, and you can go to sleep. You'll feel more like it tomorrow."

Once the tangles were worked out, he wrapped my hair, squeezing the excess moisture out through the towel. He lifted me to put my feet on the floor and replaced the damp towel around me with a dry one. It was more like a beach towel, covering me from armpits to knees and wrapping around me more than once.

I thought he'd lead me to the bedroom then, but instead he lifted me into his arms and carried me. There was an older woman in the room. She was thin and wiry with sun-leathered skin and long gray hair kept in a thick braid down her back. A look of concern was on her face as she approached us.

"Put her on the bed, Deadeye." Her tone was authoritative, like she was used to being obeyed. He set me down before brushing a kiss on my forehead, then stepped back. The woman sat on the edge of the bed next to me, giving me a kind smile. "They call me Mama. I was a doctor in another life. An Army surgeon. Now, I try to help out where I can. Me and Pops took this bunch in like they were our own. That includes you now." She reached for my chin, gently tilting my head back, turning it this way and that, obviously getting a look at the bruising on my neck. When she finished, she looked away with a scowl. "I know of one child of mine who's gettin' a spankin'," she muttered.

"I promised her I'd give him a beatin'." Deadeye leaned against the wall, one arm resting on his hip. He had a towel wrapped around his waist, but that was it. And, oh, my God, the man was seriously built!

The muscles over his chest and abdomen were thick and defined. His arms and shoulders powerful. Prominent veins ran under his skin in a sexy display, a testament to how fit he was. I couldn't help but remember the kiss he'd given me earlier. It had been the most erotic event of my life, and I wanted more. Now more than ever. I wanted to know what it was like to have his body work mine into a frenzy. I knew he could do it easily. Just looking at him made me hot and uncomfortable. Now, I knew what all the fuss was about. Any sexual attraction I'd thought I'd experienced before was nothing compared to the pull I had toward the man calling himself Deadeye.

"Aren't you going to get dressed?" To my embarrassment, my voice was nothing more than a squeak.

Deadeye gave a low chuckle. "I'll get dressed when you get dressed. Mama has to look you over first, so I'll wait. We'll get dressed together."

For some reason, that struck me as considerate when it really shouldn't have. He was practically naked. As was I. But it just felt like he knew I was uncomfortable and was showing solidarity. It was just a small thing, but it made me feel like he was throwing himself in there with me. Like we were a team or something. Which was silly. But I really wanted it to be that way, and once my mind seized on the notion, I was stuck with it.

Mama was gentle and didn't expose me or embarrass me in any way. She just made sure I wasn't hurt and that I was rebounding now that I had warmed up. I was still chilled, but I felt better. More alert. My mind wasn't nearly as fuzzy as it had been, but I was exhausted.

"I think you'll be fine." Mama smiled as she stood, patting my knee as she did. "If that ankle gives you trouble let me know. You were lucky, young lady. Thankfully there were three talented hunters tracking you and one very strong, very stubborn, very regretful man able to lift that log off you."

I looked over at Deadeye. "Sword?"

He nodded. "Yeah, baby. He was out the window with me from the very moment I realized you'd run."

That both surprised me and made me feel bad. I'd written him off. But, I mean, he'd nearly strangled me to death!

"I'm grateful." I was ashamed to admit it, but that was as much as I could manage at the moment.

Mama smiled. "I'll let Deadeye know the extent of Sword's injuries tomorrow. He's currently in my clinic waiting for me to finish with you. Do you mind if I let him know you're OK? He's done nothing but ask after you, and the man *is* in a lot of pain."

"He has?" I looked away. I wasn't sure what I was supposed to feel, but I was at rock bottom. "Probably wants to know if he needs to finish the job." I hadn't really meant to say that out loud, but the second I did I regretted it. "I'm sorry. That was petty." I'd been fighting tears for hours now. Since Sword had attacked me. Now, I knew I'd reached my limit. Despite still trying to fight them off, the tears came. I swiped at them angrily, but they still fell. "I'm sorry." The little sob that escaped couldn't be helped. I was on the verge of losing my self-control. When that happened, I wanted everyone away from me.

"Honey, you have every right to feel the way you do." Mama patted my shoulder. "Don't give in to him too easily. He needs to work for it. More than one of the men in this club has vowed to kick his ass, and his ol' lady has kicked him out of the house until he makes things right with you. Seems he can't decide if he's going to camp outside his house on the porch or outside Deadeye's door where he knows you are."

"You're talking like it's a forgone conclusion I'll just let bygones be bygones. I'm not sure I can do that. Once I'm able, I fully intend to leave here."

"Give me time, honey." Again, Deadeye had been so still and silent, I'd nearly forgotten he was in the room. My gaze snapped to his. He had a little grin on his face, but still didn't move. "I'll get you to want to stay here. With me."

"Just so." Mama nodded crisply as if that were her final say in the matter. "Get some sleep. Let your man fuss over you for a while. You'll feel much better in the morning."

"He's not my man, you know."

"Oh?" Mama looked from me to Deadeye with a knowing look. "Might want to tell that to him." With a wave, Mama left us, closing the door behind her.

* * *

Deadeye

Yeah. Mama had my number. I was gone on Chloe already. I hadn't really been in her company long at all. A couple hours maybe? But I already knew she was going to be mine. The second Mama left, I went to my dresser and got a pair of sleep pants for me and one of my T-shirts for Chloe. Thankfully, the women had come through for her and brought a backpack full of necessary items. Pants, shirts, socks, and two new packs of underwear. Among other things, including pajamas. I fished out the underwear and tossed her the unopened pack along with my shirt. I could have given her the pajamas, but I wanted her in my clothing.

"Thanks." Her husky whisper did wicked things inside me. I wanted her desperately, but I wanted her to feel safe and comfortable more. Right now, she was neither.

"Just toss your towels in the general direction of the bathroom. I'll get 'em in a minute." I didn't leave the room, but turned my back to her, dropping my towel and sliding on the soft cotton pants. I knew my cock was at attention but decided to ignore it. She was bound to see it sooner or later. Besides, I was going to be good tonight. Mostly.

"Thanks, Deadeye. I would have died out there if not for you and Sword." Her voice had me tied up in knots. The husky sound was sexy, like she'd been screaming my name during bout after bout of hot, sweaty, nasty sex. Unfortunately, it was really that way because Sword had nearly strangled her. Working through all that in my mind was going to take a while.

"Goose helped, too. You'll meet him tomorrow."

"Goose?"

"Yeah. Been my best friend and had my back my entire life. He'll have your back now, too."

"You realize you sound nuts, right?" She gave me a little smile, and I thought I'd been visited by an angel. The girl was an absolutely stunning beauty. No way this Sting guy didn't come after her. Any man would fight to keep her. Luckily, I was fucking good in a fight.

"Why? You're part of us. Were the second we realized you were Sword's daughter." I thought about that a moment. "No. You were part of us the second you admitted you were here for our help."

"Sword didn't think so." She looked away, taking my sunshine. God, I was pathetic!

"Sword can be an ass. Doesn't excuse what he did, but I can tell you the man regrets it. Why did he react like he did? No clue. But I'll find out. He'll still get a beating, no matter his reasoning. And I don't mean by just me either. He has to answer to Cain and the rest of the club."

"Hasn't he already? Cain didn't do anything to him." She shrugged. "I mean, I don't really want anything to happen to him. If he spent much time with my mother, then I understand his reaction. At least, partially. She's a piece of work, Deadeye. Her superpower is manipulation, and she's the best there is. Doesn't mean I want to be around him. Just... let it go. I'll leave, and no one will have to give this incident another thought."

I shook my head. "That's where you're wrong, Chloe. We police our own. There is a way things are done in this club. Everyone here has known each other for years. There are a few newer members, but we worked together long before we were part of Bones. What Sword did violates everything we stand for. He knows it, too. He'll lose standing in the club before this is over, and he'll accept it willingly."

"Right." She snorted as she settled herself back against the pillows at the headboard. The covers were around her hips, covering her so she sat there in my big shirt. The neckline slipped down over one shoulder, but she didn't seem to notice. The sleeves came past her elbows. "I wasn't around my stepdad's club much, but one thing I know about MCs is that you never show weakness. No way Sword accepts any kind of reprimand without protest. Not when he believes he's in the right. If my mother manipulated him the same way she does everyone else, he'll firmly believe he was in the right."

"Maybe you'd be right if it had been your mother he'd strangled. But he didn't. He strangled *you*. You'd never met him before, right?"

"No. I hadn't." One tear slipped from her cheek, and it nearly gutted me. I could already tell I hated her tears. She'd been holding back for the most part, but she needed to let it out. The problem was, when she did, it was going to be a special kind of hell for me. And it might make me unleash on Sword quicker than

I should.

"You're not your mother, Chloe. Doesn't matter if you look like her or not. You're not your mother. Sword knew that. He knows he fucked up."

She swiped at her cheek, dashing away the tear. "Whatever."

I sat on the bed next to her. When she didn't immediately turn back to me, I reached for her chin, gently turning her head toward me with my fingers. "Look at me, Chloe. Really listen to me." When she met my gaze, her eyes swimming with tears, her chin quivering, I felt like I'd been punched in the balls. "Fuck." I shook my head a little, trying to shake off the need to kill my brother. "Sword will be taken care of. Yes, he's our brother. He's a long-time member of Bones with a high position in the club. You might think his transgressions won't matter, but his status as Enforcer of Bones makes them even worse. He's the one who's supposed to prevent shit like that from happening. If it does, he's the one who's supposed to punish the transgressors. Cain will bring it up in Church and Sword *will* be punished. His punishment will not only match the crime, but his position in the club will make that punishment even worse."

She shrugged, trying to look away, but I wouldn't let her. "It doesn't matter, Deadeye. It's done. It's over. I'm fine. I just want…" She took a shuddering breath. "I just…"

That was all I could stand. I pulled Chloe into my arms and held her close. She didn't even try to push away. Just wrapped her arms around me and clung, her face pressed into my bare chest while she sobbed like her heart was breaking.

I just let her cry it out. I'd known this was coming, but the reality was so much worse than I'd expected. Each tear, each heart-wrenching sob, hardened my resolve to kill Sword. When she finally pulled away and just primal-screamed, I realized her grief was way more than she'd ever let on. This woman had truly thought her daddy would save her and was now faced with a reality where her daddy might just be the monster she should run away from instead of toward.

"I swear to you, Chloe, I'll fix this." I found myself giving her reassurances I had no idea if I could follow through with, but I damn sure intended to try. Starting with taking my grievances to Church.

It took her a while to get it all out, but I stayed with her through it all. When she'd finally worn herself out, she lay with her head on my chest, clinging to me like I was her lifeline. It took a little bit, but she finally drifted off to sleep. When she did, I rolled us over to spoon her. She went willingly, settling against me before she was still. Once her breathing was deep and even, I carefully extracted myself, tucking the covers around her securely.

I dressed quickly, keeping an eye on Chloe. If she woke, I'd get her back to sleep before I left her, because I wasn't taking a chance on her trying to bail again. Or, more importantly, her being here miserable without me. She didn't wake, thankfully. Poor thing had to be exhausted. I doubt she'd slept much since she'd left her home.

Leaving quietly, I found Sword outside our room looking grim as he met my gaze. "You heard?" If he did, then he knew what was coming. No man worth anything could have listened to Chloe grieving and not been affected.

"I did."

I nodded and turned to head down the hall,

knowing Sword would follow. Goose would have an eye on Chloe so she couldn't leave without me knowing exactly when she left and which way she went, but I was hoping she'd give me a chance to prove I'd protect and defend her like she deserved.

Cain was in his office looking over a stack of papers. Data and Zora were on the couch, Zora perched on Data's lap while the two explained what they'd found in their search of Iron Tzars MC.

"Chloe was right in that they wear the one percent patch, but that appears to refer to their methods of dealing with stuff they don't much like. They're vigilantes, Cain. Bounty hunters on the surface, but they deal in some really dark messes." Data laid it out for Cain in a matter-of-fact manner. "Nothing has ever been linked to them, but there are rumors in the biker communities around them. They've busted up more than one small-time trafficking ring. They seem to work at policing their immediate area but have ventured out farther when there's a need."

"They take jobs?" Cain continued to flip through the papers on his desk.

"You mean like mercenaries? No." Data shook his head firmly. "Any killing they do is deserved. Murderers. Child molesters. Serial killers. Serial rapists. The worst of the worst, Cain. They've taken out a few guys who repeatedly beat their women. Anyone they go after disappears."

"Any indication they're after Chloe?" When Cain looked up, he was the commander I served and followed. The commander who was ready to lead us all into battle. For my woman. If my loyalty hadn't already been firmly with Cain, it would have been in that moment.

"Yeah." Zora spoke softly before turning her head back to Data's chest and rubbing her cheek against him. He kissed the top of her head before she continued. "They're headed straight to us. Sting is personally leading his team. I don't know if they know she's here or if they know Sword's her father and are coming to enlist his help. But they're coming."

Cain shook his head once, obviously not liking something. Probably the speed of how this was happening. As a rule, Bones was always ready for anything, but Cain didn't like not knowing everything about an approaching enemy. "ETA?"

Data shrugged. "I'd say later this evening or tomorrow depending on if they want to case out the place. Want me to reach out to them?"

"Yes. Ask what they intend to do in our territory. If they say they're coming for a target, tell them to give us the information and we'll take care of it."

"On it, Prez." Data lifted Zora off his lap and stood. "I'll let you know the second I hear something."

Cain turned his attention to me. "How is she?"

I shrugged. "As well as can be expected." I looked over my shoulder. Sure enough, Sword was right behind me. He sighed and stepped fully into the room but kept silent. "I think it all hit her. She had a good scream and cry, then passed out." I glanced at Sword. "She still intends to leave. I'm doing my best to make her feel safe, but she has the bruises to prove otherwise."

"Yeah." The president scrubbed a hand over his face and turned his chair away from us. "Fuck."

"Prez, I'm turnin' in my Enforcer patch. Stepping down. I'll accept whatever punishment you hand down, but I'd respectfully request you keep Magenta and the kids under the club's protection."

Cain spun around fast and jumped to his feet, pounding the desk once with his fist. "Motherfuck! What the fuck were you thinking, Sword?" Cain looked angrier than I'd ever seen the man. Even angrier than he had when he'd punched Sword after the incident. "Not only did you traumatize an innocent woman, but your *own wife* is suffering because of what you did!"

"Fully aware," Sword said, looking down at the floor. "I hurt her as badly as I did Chloe. Brought back memories of the club she came from and her mother."

"If El Diablo comes up here to get his daughter, I'm not standing in his way. And if he decides to take her pain out on your flesh, that's on you. Bones will not lift a finger to stop him. Get me?"

"Noted." Sword looked like a broken man. He was definitely punishing himself for what he'd done, and it was obvious he regretted the incident. Not that it would help him much.

"I want it understood that Chloe is under my protection now." I'd said as much before, but I wanted Cain's blessing with this. "She's in my room now, and I have Goose watchin' over her. I intend for her to stay there, though we haven't really gotten that far. I think I've made a positive impression on her, though. We got off to a bit of a rocky start, but she let me hold her while she grieved. I can get her to stay willingly given enough time." I looked at Sword. "But he's got to be dealt with, Cain. I want to take this up in Church, with your permission."

"Oh, make no mistake. This matter will definitely be taken to Church. I'll leave it up to the club what happens next, Sword, but you're on the bubble. You get kicked out, I'll give Magenta the choice of what she wants to do. If she chooses to stay here, we'll protect her and her children with the full weight of the club. If she chooses to go to Florida to Black Reign and her father, we'll make sure they all get there safely." He leaned over the desk, his hands resting flat on the surface as he glared at Sword. "Because *we do not hold the family accountable for the actions of the dumbasses related to them.*" He enunciated each word carefully to get his point across. Sword had the good grace to wince as he looked away from our president. "You're confined to quarters until further notice. If Magenta doesn't want you at the house, you can have your old room back. But you will remain there until I can get Church called."

"What if the Iron Tzars come before then?" Sword's voice was quiet and respectful even as he demanded to be in that fight.

"You'll stay in your fuckin' room. No exceptions."

"But --"

"Goddammit, Sword!" He pounded his desk with his fist again. "I'm done talkin' to you." Cain dismissed him with a wave of his hand before snapping. "Go. Get your ass to your quarters. Now! Before I decide to just put a bullet in your brain and be done with it!"

Surprisingly, Sword only nodded before leaving. I raised my eyebrow, not sure how to proceed in the face of Cain's wrath.

"Just fuckin' say what you want to say, Deadeye." Cain sat back down in his chair, looking like the weight of the world was on his shoulders.

"I want first go at him," I demanded. "I owe it to Chloe because I should have done a better job protecting her."

"You had no idea Sword would react like he did.

This is all on him."

"I'd like to know why he had such a visceral reaction to her."

Cain snorted. "You and me both." He scrubbed a hand over his face. "Once Data and Zora have an idea of what the Iron Tzars want with Chloe and know exactly where they are and how fast they're traveling, I'll call Church. Until then, I suggest you lock down your woman. Make her understand you're solidly in her corner."

"I'm all over that, Prez. Gonna take time, though. Don't even like leaving her to meet with you, but it had to be done."

"Yeah. Make sure she has Angel's number. Should be programmed into the phone the women put in her welcome pack but double-check. I don't want her feeling like she has no one other than you. The women are going to be crucial to her trusting us."

"Will you have Angel ask Magenta to come see her? I think maybe seeing how distraught Magenta is might help reassure her this is not how we treat our women."

"If Magenta's not too traumatized her own damned self. She's pretty pissed from what Angel says. Pissed and hurt. Their son's especially upset. He's the main reason Sword isn't allowed back in the house. Kid was in the common room, coming to get his mother, when it happened. He's barely a teenager but can't stand to see his mother upset on the best of days. Hell, he's even mad at me for calling her out even though I was as gentle as I could be with Magenta."

"So, what do you want me to do?"

"I want you to calm your woman. Make sure she knows that we will not hand her over to another club unless she wants to go. She's one of us now. Reassure her however you can."

"Ain't gonna be easy. But it's going well so far. I'm serious, though. I intend to make her my ol' lady." I leveled my gaze on Cain, giving him a steady look so he knew I meant business. This wasn't a decision made out of defiance to Sword or even some whim because I felt sorry for Chloe. I was dead serious and wanted Cain to appreciate the fact.

"I hear you, brother. And yes. If Sword's punishment includes a beatin', you'll get first go. I'll let Bohannon know so he doesn't get his panties in a wad."

I gave a crisp nod. "Good. I'll go back to Chloe. I'd like to be kept in the loop about the issue with Iron Tzars, if you don't mind." I was careful not to phrase my request as a demand even though that was essentially what it was.

Cain snorted. "Yeah. I hear you. You can tiptoe your way around authority better than just about anyone I know. Just don't think I'm letting you bully me into getting what you want. You're her man. You need to know. That's all this is about."

"As long as I get my way in this, I could give a fuck if I bully you or not."

That got a bark of laughter from Cain. He looked like he'd needed the brief humor. I imagine there was a heavy weight on his shoulders. I know there was on mine. Sword had been part of the club and a trusted brother as long as I had. And I'd been in Bones for more than twenty years.

"Get on, you. Go back to your woman and leave me the fuck alone." His grin belied his gruff words and tone. I sketched him a two-finger salute before turning and following his instructions.

Chapter Five

Chloe

I woke up surrounded in warmth to the most comforting and amazing smell. Autumn rain. Pine. That faint smell after you've been asleep in a warm, comfortable bed. Cozy. I stretched, and a deep, masculine groan accompanied strong arms tightening around me. I didn't feel restricted. Just... wanted. Cared for.

"Deadeye?"

"Yeah, baby. I'm here."

I had my head on his chest, my hand clutching his side. I wasn't sure exactly what had happened, but I was torn between mortified and titillated. No doubt he'd expect sex. What man wouldn't after waking up in this position? But the more I thought about it, the less I was opposed to it. I wasn't sure I was brave enough to actually admit out loud I wouldn't mind sex with him, but I wouldn't rebuff him either.

"Um, I don't remember how I got in this specific position."

His chuckle warmed my insides and sounded way too damned good for my peace of mind. "I doubt you do. You were exhausted."

"I'm not trying to be snippy or anything. I'm just genuinely puzzled. Did I tell you to sleep with me?"

"No. But I didn't want you getting the idea you could run off again. Besides, I enjoyed myself. Tell me it bothered you waking up in my arms, and I'll leave you alone." I thought about lying. "And before you lie to me, know there will be consequences."

"Wait. What?"

"You heard me." Again, he chuckled softly. "So, what's the verdict, girl?"

I sighed. "Fine. I did like it. I've never slept with a man before. Like, actually *slept*. It was a little disorienting at first, but I can't say it was a bad experience. Besides, I don't remember even falling asleep."

He grinned, and the effect was devastating. Though his beard hid some of his features, his smile softened some of the hard planes of his face. Laugh lines fanning out around his eyes gave him one more sexy touch. Yeah. I had no defenses against Deadeye. "Good. I'll make sure you sleep with me all the time, then."

"You're a strange individual, Deadeye." I couldn't help but laugh. This was the kind of man I wanted in my life. The kind of man I wanted to stay with. To be fair, I hadn't really given Sting a chance, but I wasn't interested in leaving Deadeye now that I was here.

"Isaac."

"What?"

"My name, baby. Isaac Julian. Just make sure you call me Deadeye in front of people. I have a certain reputation to uphold." He scowled at me, and I surprised myself by giggling.

"There's that sound I love so much," he said roughly. "I'm going to kiss you, Chloe. If you don't want it, tell me now. Won't hurt my feelings. I won't be pissed or anything. But I want to kiss you."

I nodded my head, looking up at him. "Yes," I whispered. "Please."

He pulled me to him, careful not to move too fast. He let me have time to change my mind, but that wasn't going to happen. I wanted it. Needed it. The second our lips met, I sighed and leaned into him. My arms went around his neck, and I let him pull me on top of him completely.

I straddled his hips when he guided me there, rubbing my body over his deliciously muscled one. The way his arms felt wrapping around me was a heaven I'd never known. I felt safe. Comforted. It felt like, as long as I was in his arms, this man would protect me. Deadeye. Isaac.

He licked the seam of my lips, and I obediently opened for him. When he swept his tongue into my mouth, I shivered, a little whimper escaping. I arched my hips, rubbing over the erection pressing insistently against me.

"Oh, God!" Deadeye swallowed my cry, answering me with a satisfied grunt. His hands slid to my ass, squeezing and kneading the fleshy globes. The move pulled another moan from me.

"I love the sounds you make, Chloe." He sounded supremely satisfied. As if this was exactly the response he wanted from me.

"Deadeye --"

"Isaac, baby. When I'm makin' love to you, I want you to call me Isaac."

"Yes. Isaac."

He rolled us over, settling on top of me so that his weight pressed me into the mattress. I thought having a man's weight on top of me so solidly would be uncomfortable at the very least. Maybe even claustrophobic. But it felt right. Made me hungry for what I knew Isaac could give me.

"How far do you want to take this, Chloe? I won't hurt you, and I won't fuck you without your permission. Much as I want you, I know this is fast. Have you had sex before?" He looked into my eyes, his fingers tangling in my hair.

I gave him a startled bark of laughter. "How can

you possibly ask me that now?"

He shrugged. "Well, it's better than not askin' at all, baby. I'll give you as much pleasure as I can. I'll make it good for you."

"Oh, I have no doubt you will. And if you stop, I might have to smother you with a pillow while you sleep."

Deadeye -- Isaac -- kissed me again as he chuckled. "I got you, baby. Now, tell me how much experience you've had. I don't want to hurt you."

"Yeah," I muttered. "This isn't embarrassing or anything."

"There's no shame in this, Chloe. I ain't judging at all. I just need to make sure I don't hurt you."

"Mom kept a tight rein on me. I think I was her insurance policy. Trade the little virgin to someone for whatever favor she wanted. I haven't been with a man, but I penetrated myself..." I trailed off, my face flaming as I looked away. "Is that weird?"

"Honey, nothing you do to pleasure yourself is weird. If it's what you need, you go for it. I'll be careful, but you need to understand that I'm not taking this back. I intend to keep you, Chloe. That means you stay here. With me."

I stiffened. "I'm not staying here with Sword. I understand he made sacrifices to help rescue me, but it doesn't change the fact he tried to kill me."

"Sword's in a world of trouble, honey. I'm not sure he'll survive with his club membership intact when Cain is done with him. And yeah. He's earned a beatin' he'll be taking before he goes."

"I never meant to cause trouble for him. I just... I needed help..."

"And you did exactly what you should have done. You went to your dad for help. It's on him he was a stupid-ass motherfucker."

That made me giggle, which earned me a sexy grin from Isaac. "That really shouldn't have been funny."

"Sure, it was. The point is, let me worry about Sword. I've got your back. You're gonna be mine, and I will keep anything and everything away from you. I know it seems a lot like you're jumping from one bad situation to another, but if you're my ol' lady, it will signal to any other club looking to make trouble that you're my property. Any biker worth his salt will protect his property to the death. I'll order you a cut and a patch. We'll have it in a couple of days. Then, we'll be in a much better position with Iron Tzars."

"I tried to pretend I had a choice, Isaac. I can see now that was all wishful thinking. So, if this is the way it has to be, I choose you. I won't lie, though. I'm a little scared. And I won't tolerate cheating. I was always told being an ol' lady didn't necessarily mean the woman was the biker's only lover. But I couldn't take that."

"It's you and me, honey. No one else for either of us. I ain't an easy man to live with, but I swear I will do my best to always do right by you."

"Then let's do this. You tried to keep me out of the storm. You came after me when I ran. You were gentle with me when I was so fragile." I reached up and stroked his beard as I smiled at him. "You make me feel safe."

"From now on, that's my job, honey. I'll make you feel safe and make sure you *are* safe." He kissed me again. "We'll make this work, Chloe. I swear."

I believed him. Honestly, though, it didn't matter. Because I wanted this. I'd be his for however long he'd have me and worry about the aftermath later. I had to choose which direction my life was going. I could go back to my mother and the very place I'd run from, or I could trust myself and throw my lot in with a man who'd already proven he'd protect me. Even from myself. Yeah. No brainer.

"Yes, Isaac. Yes."

He kissed me again. His hands tunneled up my shirt to grip my breasts, and the feeling was indescribable. There was a slight bite of pain as his fingers dug into my flesh, but it was also strangely arousing. I craved that sensation. Needed it. Arching into his touch, I whimpered, bringing my hands to his and urging him to continue. I loved his weight on me. Loved the way he was so powerful. He had control, but he tempered that power. For me.

When he raised himself above me and urged my shirt up, I willingly shrugged out of it, wanting to be against him skin to skin. His hard, warm chest against my nipples was heaven, his kisses drugging. I wrapped my legs around him, holding him close. The hard ridge of his erection pressed against me, and I rubbed against it until I found the perfect angle. My clit pulsed, and I cried out into his mouth.

"Fuck, yeah." His growl was like another hand to stroke me with. I loved his voice in that particular tone. "You like that, don't you? Can feel the heat of your pussy against my fuckin' cock. Hot little thing…" His words were spoken between kisses against my mouth. He found a nipple with his fingers and pinched. The pleasure combined with the sharp pain was unexpected and overwhelming. An orgasm rushed through me so hard and sudden all I could do was suck in a breath before my body seized. My muscles locked, and I was helpless to do anything other than let the pleasure overtake me. I couldn't even cry out!

Couldn't let him know how good it felt. How he made me feel...

"My God," he whispered as he left my mouth to find my neck and suck. "You came, didn't you? I can feel your clit pulsing on my dick. Such a responsive little thing." He nipped and sucked my neck. I was sure he left his mark there. Like a brand. "Before we leave this bed, Chloe, you're gonna give me your orgasms. I won't be satisfied until you've passed out in my arms." He sucked again, making another point on my neck sting, which triggered little shivers through my body that were just shy of an orgasm. "This won't be a short romp, baby. It will take a very long time. I'm gonna know your body inside and out. What you like. What you love. And what makes you lose your fuckin' mind. Then I'm gonna take those last things and drive you mad with them. Before we leave this bed, you're gonna know you belong to me."

God help me, I believed him. Isaac -- Deadeye -- had my number. He was going to use my body's responses against me in the most pleasurable way. And I was going to let him.

Sweat erupted over my skin at his words and wicked love bites. My body trembled at his touch. I was wound so tight it was uncomfortable, and I knew I needed more than that one powerful orgasm to ease it. I also had a feeling I wasn't getting relief any time soon. If he could give me an orgasm like that, more powerful than anything I'd known by my own hand, and I still needed more, there was no way I was going to keep my sanity. I was fully at his mercy. It was enough that I should have been sent into a panic. He could easily control me with my own sexuality. Manipulate me like my mother manipulated the people in her life. The control Isaac could wield over me was tremendous. Yet, I wasn't fighting back. I was willingly giving him this power over me. And I was fully embracing it.

* * *

Deadeye

The moment Chloe surrendered, I took full control. At least, I thought I did. The reality was, I knew she had just as much control over me as I did over her. Part of me embraced it. A relationship was nothing if not give and take. I was essentially taking over her life. Her future. It was only fair I give her the same.

Her body was a fucking paradise. Everywhere I touched her seemed to trigger sexual endorphins or something inside her. The more I explored, the more she whimpered and moved, trying to get friction where she needed it most. She thrust her chest at me when I kissed my way down her neck and chest to latch onto a nipple. The harder I sucked, the more she moaned. Her fingers tunneled in my hair and gripped tightly. Sweat slickened her skin as her cries increased. I knew when I finally made it to her pussy she'd be drenched and ready for anything I wanted to do to her.

"Isaac!" Her strangled cry was the sweetest music, her breathing ragged and labored. She looked up at me, a crazed look of wonder on her face. "What are you doing to me?"

"Eating you alive, baby." I gave her a wicked grin. "Eating you a-fucking-live." I bit down on her nipple, tugging slowly, watching her face as the pleasure morphed into just the tiniest bit of pain.

Her eyes widened a fraction, and her lips formed an "O" of surprise. The second I saw I'd pushed her into the realm of more pain than pleasure, I released the little nub. She screamed my name, and her body shuddered beneath me once again. God! Her body was a playground of sensation. I felt like a kid at a birthday party, unsure which present to open first. Everywhere I kissed, licked, or nipped seemed to set her off.

"Has no one ever touched you before, Chloe?" I purred the question, trying to keep her in the moment even as I interrogated her. I should have found out more about her experience other than if she was a virgin or not.

"No!" She cried out her answer, sounding as desperate as I was becoming. "Never! Oh, God! Don't stop! Please!"

If her immediate and aggressive answer hadn't spiked my own lust, I'd have chuckled. But all I could do was what she demanded of me. I continued to play with her glorious tits. The small mounds were perky, the nipples hard pebbles from my attentions and her desire. I rubbed my face against her chest, letting my beard caress her. The different sensations seemed to fuel her fire even more. Chloe cried out sharply, bucking beneath me as I continued to kiss and suck her breasts. God! This woman was perfect! There were no reservations in her reaction. She just let them come, welcoming my attentions as I moved down her body inch by slow inch.

I brushed the undersides of her breasts with kisses and licks, teasing her delicate abdomen with kisses, brushing my beard against her skin just as a different sensation so she never got used to one thing. She was always on edge, never knowing if I'd lick or bite her skin. By the time I wedged my shoulders between her legs, Chloe was a writhing, screaming mass of nerves. And she'd never looked more beautiful.

"My God..." Looking up at her as her body sweated and wept for me was the most awe-inspiring vision I'd ever seen. She was mad with lust, with her need. Of me. I wanted nothing more than to mount her. Fuck her sweet little pussy until we both passed out. And I would. Just not yet. I wanted her to be solidly mine. I'd done my best to prove I'd look out for her and keep her safe. Now I had to prove I could pleasure her better than her wildest imaginings. And I wanted my kid in her belly. That would tie us together better than anything else I could do. "You are the most exquisite creature I've ever seen, Chloe. Absolutely beautiful in every single way."

"Isaac." Her breathy whisper, her voice catching. "Please."

"My pleasure, baby." Then I lowered my face to her glistening pussy and took a long swipe with my tongue. I wasn't sure who was more surprised by the contact, her or me. She jerked and gave a sharp, startled cry before screaming my name at the top of her lungs. Her sweet taste hit me like a shot of adrenaline straight to the heart. I groaned in defeat, fastening my mouth around her pussy so I covered both her opening and her clit. Her juice was like honeyed nectar as I lapped it up. The more I licked her, the more I was rewarded. Her little clit twitched under my tongue, pulsing with each contraction as she came.

Once she stilled, I gave her clit one last kiss. She jerked and sucked in a sharp breath, whimpering at my touch on the oversensitized nub. Instinct was driving me hard. I had to make an unbreakable tie between us. Plus, I just wanted her to be mine. There was just something about her spunk, her determination that I found not only sexy as hell, but necessary to be my woman. I'd never met anyone like her, and I knew I never would. So, this was it for me.

I brushed my beard up her body, stroking her with just that little bit more sensation. She reacted with a shiver and reached for me with her arms. Wrapping her arms around my neck, she pulled me to her for a kiss. Her lips met mine eagerly, demanding. I gave her what she wanted, plunging my tongue into her mouth and lapping at hers. She followed, mimicking my movements as she became more comfortable in participating. Well, that or she was just too turned-on to care. Either was all right with me.

I settled myself between her thighs, her legs going around my waist, her heels digging into my ass. As I continued to kiss her, my cock found her entrance, and I paused, needing to look into her eyes as I entered her.

"Look at me, Chloe. Look into my eyes. Focus on me."

"What…" She shook her head slightly, probably to clear it. "Did I do something wrong?"

"No, baby. Exactly the opposite. You're doing everything right. But I want you to look at me. Listen to what I'm going to say to you."

"O-OK." She looked adorably confused and I had to kiss her once more before I continued.

"I'm takin' you bare, Chloe. I ain't given' you a choice 'cause I'm a fuckin' bastard. I'm clean. You can check with Mama when we're finished, but I'm doin' this. I'm gonna come deep in your pussy this time and every single time I fuck you after this."

Her eyes widened. "But… Isaac. What if I get pregnant? I can't --"

I kissed her again. "You can't what, honey?"

"I can't raise a baby on my own. I don't even have a home right now."

"That's where you're wrong. First, you ain't on your own. You have me. You'll always have me. We'll have our problems, but we'll work them out. I'll be faithful to you and treat you like a fuckin' princess. You'll be faithful to me and love me with everything in you. Second, you do have a home. Here. With me. Even if you decide you hate me, you'll always have a home here. The club will always protect you." She started to shake her head, but I slid the head of my cock inside her, and her eyes widened. "I know you have reservations, so I'm going to ask you to trust me. I wouldn't say you had a home here if I didn't already know you did. As president of this club, no matter what happens to Sword or to me, Cain will always make sure you're protected and cared for. Now. Eyes on me. I'm going to slide all the way inside you, and I want to see your reaction."

"Isaac!" She sobbed my name, but widened her legs, welcoming me. "Please don't break my heart."

"Never, baby. I'm your man. And I always will be. No matter what. It's you for me." Then, with a slow, lazy glide, I slid my cock inside her to the hilt. She gripped me tightly, her sheath squeezing and spasming around me. She sucked in a breath, her eyes wide and wild before she screamed out an orgasm as her gaze clung to mine. "That's it, baby. You come on my cock as much as you like." I leaned down to suck on her earlobe and whispered into her ear. "Fuckin' come hard, baby. Make me come inside you and plant my seed there."

* * *

Chloe

I wish I could say a part of me wanted to slow down and talk this out, but the truth was I was all for this. There had never been a conversation where Isaac hinted he'd be faithful until we went our separate ways. He was talking like we were in a real relationship. Even so far as to tell me he was taking me as his ol' lady. I was still new to the MC culture, but my impression was that taking an ol' lady was a serious thing. A biker didn't do it unless he intended to be with her long term. My own mother had been ol' lady to a biker and, even when she manipulated him so much he opted to retire from being president, he still didn't throw her over. They were still together as of a week ago when I left. If ever there was a cause for a guy to leave his woman, I'd say my mother's meddling in club business would qualify.

But he hadn't left. He'd resigned his position as president instead. It told me a lot about Warlock as a man. The fact that Iron Tzars hadn't taken matters into their own hands and done something horrible to both Warlock and my mother -- perhaps even me by extension -- told me a lot about the club as well.

So, when Isaac slid himself into me without a condom, telling me in no uncertain terms he was never using a condom with me, I should have protested. But I didn't. Instead, I embraced it. Embraced Isaac Julian and everything he represented. I spread my legs wider, giving him permission to do as he wanted.

"Yes," I whispered. "I want that, Isaac. Want you to come inside me."

"You'll carry my child? Stay with me and let me protect you both?"

I nodded. "Yes. And I'll protect you both, too."

"Good. Now." He moved inside me. One stroke out, then back in. "I'm gonna make you come. And you're gonna take me with you."

When Isaac started moving, my breath caught.

The pleasure resumed like he'd never stopped. Maybe I was just that greedy for him. I was beginning to wonder how I'd ever lived without sex this long in my life.

Isaac built the pleasure inside me with expert ease. It wasn't long before I'd wrapped my legs around him again and met him thrust for thrust. I grunted and strained, needing him to go faster. Harder. I wanted to verbalize my needs but couldn't seem to get the words out.

"Please! Oh, God! Isaac!"

"You need more, baby?" His mouth found the side of my neck and he sucked, making yet another mark of possession on my skin.

"Yes! Fuck me hard!" My words were nothing more than a needy whimper, but Isaac complied with my demand.

He surged inside me, our flesh slapping together loudly. I thought he might flip me over or something to be in complete control, but he just flexed his hips with hard, quick snaps. Not long after he set the harder, faster pace, I felt my orgasm building inside me. I wanted to fight it off, to make this last as long as I possibly could, but I was just too inexperienced, the sensations too strong.

With a shrill cry, I came, clinging tightly to Isaac. His own yell of completion followed soon after, but I could barely hear him for the roaring in my ears. Vaguely, I knew he kissed and praised me. Why, I could only imagine. I hadn't really done anything. Just gave myself to him to use as he pleased. When I was still, when the blood gradually flowed back to my brain for rational thought, I realized Isaac was still on top of me, his cock still firmly inside me.

"You good, baby?" He combed his fingers

through my hair gently, petting me as he kissed my cheek and the marks on my neck he'd put there.

"I think so." I was suddenly so sleepy I could barely hold my eyes open. I'd had more than one orgasm and my body, though sweaty and sticky, was worn out.

"Let's get you in the shower to wash off the sweat, then we'll rest." He bent and kissed me gently. I sighed into the kiss, wondering if I could get him to repeat what we'd just done.

He chuckled. "Greedy for me again, baby?"

"If I said yes, would you still respect me?"

That got a bark of laughter from him. "Oh, yeah. I'll always respect you. Especially if you continue to want me this much. I just don't want you to be too sore."

"But I'm not."

"You will be later. Don't worry, though. I'll kiss it better."

I groaned. "You can't say stuff like that and expect me to keep my hands to myself." I was only half joking.

"No one said I expected you to keep your hands to yourself. Feel free anytime you want." With one last kiss, he stood, scooping me up as he did. Then he carried me to the bathroom where he started the shower and stepped in with me.

He washed me carefully, especially between my legs. Then he knelt in front of me and licked my pussy, paying close attention to my clit. That led to shower sex, which led to him having to wash me again.

"Fuck." Isaac leaned against me after he'd come inside me again, this time with me pressed against the shower wall, my body trapped between the wall and his hard body.

"Yeah. We did that." I giggled weakly.

"I didn't hurt you, did I? I was rougher with you than I intended to be."

"No, Isaac." I turned, cupping his cheek and pulling him to me for a kiss. "It was perfect. If I never get to have sex ever again, you've made these experiences good enough to last a lifetime."

He pulled me into his arms. "We'll definitely be having sex again. Every day for the rest of our lives if I have anything to say about it. When I'm old and can't get it up, I'll eat you out until you beg for mercy."

"Don't let anyone tell you you're not romantic." For the first time since my mother had taken me to the Iron Tzar's compound to meet Sting, I felt like I had a happy future ahead of me. "Can I tell you something and you not freak out or get mad?"

He pulled back, reaching for a towel to wrap around my shoulders. He snagged another one to start drying me with. "You can tell me anything. I can't tell you how I'll react without knowing the content of the conversation, but I can promise to always talk it out with you."

I nodded. I really couldn't expect anything more. "I kind of hope I am pregnant. My last period was two weeks ago, so it's entirely possible."

"Honey, I did this with every intention of getting you pregnant. It gives me a better claim on you when Iron Tzars come for you."

"The first thought I had was that I should stop you. I'm not on birth control and am probably ovulating right now. But I didn't. I thought that if I was pregnant, you'd have to keep me because a man like you doesn't walk out on his kid. You might leave me, but not a baby."

He sighed and pulled me into his arms. "Honey,

we both had reasons for this. None of them was out of love or a desire to have a child simply to have a family. I'm not saying I love you. I know you don't love me. But we've got chemistry and mutual respect. It's a foundation to build on."

"OK." I sighed, vowing to myself I'd always be honest with him, no matter if it hurt or scared me.

"Now. Let's get some breakfast." He gave me a cheeky grin. "I've worked up an appetite."

I couldn't help but laugh.

Chapter Six
Deadeye

"Surprisingly, they've called a halt." Data was giving his report to Cain in Church. I came in late because I'd been making sure Chloe knew she was mine. The sex had been the best of my life, and I still had a shit-eating grin on my face when I walked into the room. "They've halted just inside the city," Data went on. "Staying at a local campground until they decide what to do next."

It had been two days since I'd first claimed Chloe. She was starting to lose some of her reluctance about meeting the club members, especially the ol' ladies. They'd taken her in like one of their own, and she'd flourished under her reassurance and friendship. Even Magenta had come to meet Chloe and welcomed her with open arms. We'd all been puzzled when Iron Tzars hadn't showed yet and hadn't answered Data's messages.

"They know Chloe is here of her own free will?"

"Yes. They were headed here to get her father's help in finding her. Given his service record and his affiliation with ExFil, they thought he'd want to help in locating his daughter."

That made me angry all over again. He *should* have wanted to help locate his daughter. He should have been the one to protect her instead of me. Cain must have seen the thunderous look on my face, because he raised a hand in my direction, an order to keep silent.

"And now?"

"They still want to meet with us. Their president, a guy named Aiden Pierce. Sting. Got a decorated service record, as does his old man. Everything Chloe told us was true. Corroborated by Sting himself. At least as much as he could. Her mother arranged for a meeting between them. Sting indicated her mother wanted him to marry her daughter, though he was on the fence about it himself. He's after her now to make sure she's safe and to offer her a ride back if she wants to go home."

"He say why he ain't leaving our territory?" Cain was calm, obviously trying to get the meat of the information without the drama.

"Yeah. He wants to talk to his father. Doesn't want to make his first major decision on the fly with little to no information. Said before he leaves, he's gonna want a meet with Chloe."

My first instinct was a resounding "absolutely not." But I knew that if this club were on the up and up, they were only being certain she was OK and not in trouble. Even of her own making.

"Not unreasonable," Cain said, rubbing his finger over his upper lip. Then he looked at me. "Your woman good?"

"She is. I've put in an order with Cheetah for her property patch. She's aware and fully on board."

Sword growled but said nothing. I raised my eyebrow at him. Normally, I'd have called him out, but I wasn't the president. Or even an officer.

"Which brings me to the other matter we need to resolve." Cain stood, crossing his arms over his chest. "Sword has resigned as enforcer. Turned in his patch." Everyone kept their eyes on Cain. No one looked in Sword's direction. Which told me how high the deck was stacked against the other man. He'd be lucky if he didn't get run out of the club altogether. "I've accepted his resignation, but after careful thought, and discussion with Torpedo, I don't feel that's enough."

Torpedo picked up the thread in a show of solidarity. "We don't treat women that way. Even if they deserve it, there is a process. We're all big men. Women can be easily hurt if we can't control ourselves. It wasn't clear at the time if the girl had done wrong. Even Sword himself never offered a reason for him attacking her other than she looked like her mother."

Sword stood, his head held high. "I accept whatever punishment you see fit, including expulsion from the club."

"You're damned right you'll accept it!" Where he'd been trying to be methodical and rational during Church, Cain's fabled control slipped. He took a breath. "As of this moment, you're on probation. Your service to this club and the way you treat your woman are the only things keeping you in. We'll have a vote on whether to put you back on full duties to the club once I've had a chance to cool down and you've made your peace with Chloe. Your position depends largely on her reactions to you in the coming weeks and months."

"Not good enough," I snapped. It was the first time in my adult life I allowed my control to slip. "I promised Chloe I'd avenge her, and I will."

"You'll do what I Goddamned tell you to or you can fuckin' leave." Cain was out of patience. "I'm through being disrespected by any fucking body who decides he wants a fuckin' say. If the club wants to elect a new president, that's your right. But as long as I'm fuckin' president, you will all fuckin' respect me and my fuckin' position!"

"You knew this was comin', Cain." Torpedo gripped Cain's shoulder, but the other man shrugged him off.

"Don't give a fuck. I must be getting lax on

discipline in my old age because I've allowed too much of this shit lately." Cain pointed at me. "And you're the very last member I ever expected to challenge me. I may be a decade older than you, but I can still kick your ass, Deadeye. Don't test me!"

"He's right, Cain." Sword stood and went to the chair in the middle of the room. It was used for interrogation. Or, in this case, punishment. Sword sat down and faced the president with a steady gaze. "I deserve more than being on probation or losing my position as an officer. Deadeye promised my daughter he'd give me a beating. I'm accepting it now."

Cain sat back in his chair. "Fine. But I'm not stopping it. You give Deadeye leave to do this, he continues until he's satisfied since he's claimed Chloe as his ol' lady. And I gotta tell ya, Sword. If you'd done it to Angel, I'd kill you."

Sword just nodded. "Understood. I expect nothing less."

I have no idea how long the beating lasted, but I didn't hold back. Cain said nothing, and Sword took his punishment like a man. I think I'd have preferred if he fought back. Then I could have justified continuing. But he sat there stoically, not making a sound other than the occasional grunt.

It was Bohannon who put a hand on my shoulder. "He's had enough." Had he phrased it any other way, I'd have brushed the Sergeant at Arms aside and continued. Much as I wanted Sword to hurt for what he'd done, I didn't want to kill the man. Not really. Not with him sitting there passively as I whaled away on him.

I was breathing hard. My knuckles were scraped and bleeding almost as much as Sword's face. He was swollen and bleeding, one eye closed. The other one was glazed with pain, but he still said nothing.

"Clean up before you go to your woman." Cain's words were an order, and he was right. I didn't want to go to Chloe like this. With blood literally on my hands. It hurt more than I thought it would, too. Not physically. I could take that easily. But the pain of beating a brother. Punishing one of my own for something he never should have done.

I nodded to Cain, then turned and left the room.

* * *

Chloe

Isaac had come back to me after the club meeting with bruised knuckles and more depressed than I'd ever seen anyone. "I take it things didn't go as you'd planned?"

"Oh, they went according to plan." He pulled me into his arms. "Bastard just sat there while I beat the shit out of him. Wasn't as satisfying as I thought it would be. Which just made me angrier because you did the same thing, and he continued to assault you. God! This makes no fuckin' sense!"

"It's fine, Isaac. I'd think less of you if you enjoyed beating up someone who refused to fight back. You're a strong man. You did what you felt you had to. That doesn't mean you have to take satisfaction in it."

"No, but I honestly don't think anyone could punish Sword any more than he's punishing himself. And that just infuriates me more. He has no sense of self preservation. The only thing keeping him from leaving the club without Cain throwing him out is Magenta and his kids. He knows the club will take care of them, but he also loves them and needs to be with them." Isaac shook his head as he pulled back to look at me. "I don't know what else to do."

I wanted to cry all over again. "There's nothing more you can do. This is between Sword and me. I want so much to give this to you. To forgive and forget. I can forgive. People do things they wish they could take back. I get that. But I'm not sure I'll ever be comfortable around him."

"We can move if you want. Bones has a sister club in Palm Beach, Florida. Salvation's Bane will let me patch over if Cain gives his blessing. They're not Bones, but I know most of them from ExFil. They're good men, and I could easily make a home there."

"No. The last thing I want you to do is leave your home." I sighed, holding him close. Tears pricked at my eyes, but I wasn't going to try to manipulate him with my tears. That was what my mother would have done. "Maybe it's best if I move on, Isaac." My voice was soft. That was the last thing I wanted, but I had to put it out there.

"If you move on, Chloe, I'm moving on with you. I'm not leaving you, and I'm not letting you leave me."

"I don't want to leave, but I just can't help but feel like I've turned your life upside down. You don't need this kind of drama. No one does."

"No. But I need you, Chloe. In the short time we've known each other, you've gotten under my skin. I ain't given' you up easily. Besides, I told you when I claimed you -- this is permanent. I'm not letting you go willingly."

We clung together for a while. The thought of leaving Isaac was really more than I wanted to contemplate. The relief I felt knowing he'd taken that decision out of my hands was tremendous.

"I promised you I'd fix this, baby. Just give me time and I will. Somehow, I'll fix this."

Over the next few days Isaac made good on his

promise. He continued to put the ol' ladies in my way, and they took me under their wings, making me feel welcomed and wanted. Every time I started to feel like a burden, one of them would ask for my help, and I suddenly felt like I was part of a huge family. Amazingly, they all took my side against Sword. Even Magenta. She, more than anyone, made me feel like I not only belonged, but was wanted. She didn't try to treat me like she was my mother, but she made it clear that I would always be welcomed in her home whether or not Sword was there.

Then the day I'd been dreading came.

"They're on the move." Suzie came to me with Zora, both of them putting their arms around me, leading me inside the clubhouse. I'd been helping Magenta tend the mums she'd planted the previous month. She loved her flowers, and I was starting to understand why. Pulling out weeds and mounding mulch around the plants while spending time with the older woman was soothing, and I felt connected to her in a way I never had my own mother. She never brought up my altercation with Sword or mentioned him unless I did. When she did, she became obviously distressed, and the pain on her face was more than obvious. I could almost feel her sorrow and the way she was torn by the situation.

"Who are on the move?" I looked from Suzie to Zora in confusion.

"The Iron Tzars. They're coming with a contingent of riders. Warlock and your mother are among them."

"My mother?" I didn't resist when they took me deeper into the clubhouse, into a room with computer monitors everywhere, including one massive screen taking up an entire wall.

"Yes. From what we can tell, she's the one insisting they come after you. The communication was intentionally sent to us by Iron Tzars. I guess it was their way of giving us a heads-up. Sting went along out of respect for his father but has made it clear he's treating this as Warlock's last wishes in the club, granted only because he was the former president. After this, Warlock is leaving Iron Tzars for good."

"Wow. That club was his entire life." This was hard to take in. "It's hard enough to believe he's resigning as president -- which I heard with my own ears -- but for him to completely leave the club is like him turning his back on his family."

"It's the same here," Zora said gently. I knew what she was getting at.

I sighed. "I hear you, Zora."

"No one expects anything from you, Chloe. Don't let anyone bully you into doing something you're not comfortable with."

"Maybe I'm just scared." That admission when I knew I needed to be strong took something from me. But then, everyone here had been sacrificing for me since I'd arrived. If I didn't make an effort to put things right with Sword, I'd be just as wrong as he was. I knew better than anyone how my mother could get into someone's head. If she'd turned her attention to getting something from Sword, or getting him to do something for her, she would have been damned hard to resist. No matter what method she used.

"I understand." That came from Suzie. "When I first came here, I was afraid of everyone. Angel and Mama were the only people other than Cliff and Daniel I trusted. Probably because I'd been with a club who'd hurt me. But the way the men were with all the women, especially the women they made ol' ladies, taught me not all men liked to hurt. Then Stunner took to protecting me, and I felt even more safe. Let Deadeye take on that role for you. It will make anything uncomfortable much easier."

"I think that's the best advice I've had since I came here. And that's saying something, because I've had some really sound advice."

"This is a great bunch." Magenta squeezed my shoulder. "They've been my best friends since I came here, and I wouldn't trade them for anything in the world."

My phone buzzed in my back pocket, and I squealed, jumping at the vibration against my ass. Everyone laughed as I took it out and read the text from Isaac.

"Isaac, er, Deadeye says to stay in the control room." I glanced up at Zora. "Did you guys tell him where we were?"

"I told Data," Zora said. "No, actually, he told me if we found anything to get you and hole up in here, so I guess he told me what to do and I just let him know I'd followed his instructions." We all had a good chuckle over that too. My mood had greatly improved, even though I knew something was getting ready to go down.

"They seem to have you guys locked down." I smiled, but I really wanted to know what I was in for.

"Don't let them kid you. We do what they say with regard to safety, but we rule the roost the rest of the time." Suzie gave me a satisfied smirk.

"They love us, or they wouldn't let us get away with half the shit we do." Zora grinned. "It's part of the reason I love Data so much. He's patient and tolerant."

"Yeah? What's another reason? 'Cause he's always seemed pretty arrogant to me." Suzie looked genuinely curious.

Zora schooled her expression as she shrugged. "Sex, naturally." I loved these ladies' sense of humor. They kept me in stitches and, more importantly, distracted me when I desperately wanted to think about anything other than what was about to go down outside the compound.

"You guys are awesome," I said with a smile, meaning it from the bottom of my heart. "I appreciate you trying to distract me, but I can't leave Deadeye alone to face my problems. I need to go out there."

"You'll just divide his attention." Angel spoke from across the room near the door. "Trust me when I tell you it will be more dangerous for him if you're with him than it will be with you safely tucked away."

I sighed, looking down at my feet. Ashamed. "Out of the way."

"No." Angel moved toward me. "You'd never be in his way. You just have to understand he's a soldier. A fighter. He will always, above anything else, protect you. If you're there, he'll put himself between you and any danger. You can't protect yourself like he can. Let the boys do their jobs so everyone is safe."

"Easier said than done." I didn't like this. Not at all.

"I know, honey. Just trust me on this."

Chapter Seven
Deadeye

We met the contingent of Iron Tzars at the gate with a show of force of our own. The last thing we wanted was them inside the compound where our families were. Cain, Torpedo, and Bohannon were in agreement that if there were any lengthy discussions involved, we'd take it to the Boneyard.

"Not exactly the welcome I was expecting." The man in the lead rode a black Harley Davidson FXDR 114. Which meant the man seriously loved speed. It wasn't conventional, but it was still a Harley. I glanced at Scout on his Indian Scout. The man just smirked, as if he knew the Harley was fast, but his Scout was faster. "I'm Sting. This is Warlock and his woman, Bev."

"Where's my daughter?" Bev's question was more of a demand. Warlock squeezed her shoulder, but she shrugged him off. "She's being held here against her will, and it's your duty to get her back by any means necessary!" Bev looked up at Warlock like she fully expected him to storm the gates of hell unaided with nothing more than a squirt gun.

"Bev." He growled her name through his gritted teeth. "Let Sting handle this. He's the president."

"Only because you took the coward's way out and backed down." She sniffed her disdain.

"Control your woman, Warlock." Sting's tone was mild, but I could see his eye twitching. The man wasn't happy at all. No MC president would be in this situation. Bev was seriously overstepping her bounds, and she either didn't realize it or didn't think there would be any repercussions worth restraining herself over.

"If only," the other man muttered. "Respectfully," Warlock began. "We'd like to see Chloe. To confirm she's here on her own."

Cain shifted his stance. It was a casual move, like he was only moving weight from one leg to the other, but he'd made it easier for him to draw his gun if he needed to. "You're in no position to make demands, Warlock. You or your woman."

"We'll raze this hillbilly hellhole to the ground!" Bev snapped. She didn't move forward, just kept running her mouth like she was the queen of the club and no one would dare take her to task. And it looked like she might be right, because neither Warlock nor Sting even tried to shut her up.

"You know, my own woman is pretty outspoken when necessary." Cain rubbed his chin with his left hand. Not his dominant right hand. "If it were her daughter being held against her will, she might speak up when I told her not to. More likely, though, she'd know I was the best person for the job since I've got the military training. Well, that *and* she respects my position in the club and my ability to control it." He nodded to Bev. "Looks like you've got a problem on your hands, Warlock. It's spilling over to Sting."

Warlock nodded. "I'm aware. It's why this is my last ride with my brothers."

"We'll see." Bev flashed him a knowing look. Yeah, I could tell why Sword had issues. If this woman could manipulate her way into this man's life far enough he was willing to not only give up the presidency of his club but turn his back on his brothers, then a younger, less hardened Sword hadn't stood a chance.

"Mother, you need to leave."

If there was a God, I wished he would just shoot

me now, because that absolutely could not be Chloe coming up behind me. Sting gave me a raised eyebrow and tried to hide his smile. I saw it anyway.

"Looks like Warlock ain't the only one havin' woman troubles." Cain sighed. "She embarrasses you like Bev's doing Warlock, you're on your own, brother." I wasn't, really, but Cain had to say something.

"I'm not here to embarrass anyone." Chloe stayed behind me, taking my left hand in hers and putting her other hand on my back. She was still visible to Warlock and Bev, but I was still solidly between her and the other couple. "I just know my mother. She won't leave until she has what she wants. And she wants me." Chloe gripped my hand tighter, not letting go. "I'm not going, of course." I glanced down at her, and she smiled up at me.

"Chloe's my ol' lady." I raised my chin and put my shoulders back proudly. "She's staying with me."

"I see." That from Sting. He addressed Chloe then. "You're good with that plan? You want to stay with this guy?"

"I am. He's been good to me. The club, too."

"Bet your first meeting with your father was more than a little awkward. He on board with you staying here?" Bev's words were hateful. Like she knew exactly the number she'd done on Sword and knew he'd hate Chloe on sight. Which he kind of had.

"It was, thanks to the fact you never told him I existed."

Warlock glanced sharply at Bev. "You said he nearly beat you to death when he found out you were carrying his child.

Bev shrugged. "Water under the bridge. All that matters now is bringing Chloe home so she can be a proper woman to Sting. Your son and president of Iron Tzars."

"I never agreed to that, Bev," Sting said softly. "I was seeing where you went with the scheme, but I was never giving in to your demands simply because you demanded them. I'd considered taking her only to make sure she was safe and away from your influence. Fortunately, Chloe knows her own mind. She wanted nothing to do with any of it, so she fled." Sting grinned at Chloe. "I admire you for that, though I wish you'd talked to me in private and told me you weren't on board with your mother's plan. I'd have seen you safely away from her."

"I wasn't sure how that would work. Last thing I wanted to do was end up in a worse situation, but --" She clamped her mouth shut and looked up at me, wide-eyed. Yeah. She didn't want to out what had happened when she'd first met Sword. I wasn't sure why, but I hoped it might be to protect the other man. Or Bones. I got the feeling Sting might not take kindly to the way Sword had treated Chloe at that first meeting.

Sting looked from Chloe to me. "Problem?"

"Not now. Suffice it to say things didn't go off smoothly in the beginning. But, as you can see, Chloe is content to be here. She's my woman, and I'll take care of her."

"Chloe, come to me! Now! Stop this foolishness and come home." Bev held out her hand to Chloe like she fully expected Chloe to take it.

"I'm not going anywhere, Mom."

"Of course, you are. Right this instant."

Chloe stiffened. I glanced down at her, and her eyes flashed with anger. "I don't know what scheme you have planned, but you can count me out of it. I've been your pawn my entire life. Me and Warlock. I tried to keep my distance from him because I knew that if we formed any kind of relationship, you'd just use it against us both. He's a good person, Mother. You had a man who really loved you, and you've driven him to this. He's leaving a life he loves because he let you manipulate him. Just like you do everyone in your life. Like you did Sword. Like you did me." She shook her head, stepping away from me slightly and taking a step forward. My hackles rose slightly, but I knew she had to do this herself. Whether I liked it or not. "I'm done. You're not going to use me to get to Sting or the club." She tilted her head. "That's it, isn't it? You're after the club. Iron Tzars."

Sting's gaze snapped to Chloe. As did Cain's. "Explain," Sting snapped.

"Sword said she worked for the CIA or something when he knew her. Wanted information about Argent Tech." Data delivered the information as if he saw where Chloe was going with this. The man probably knew everything the Tzars were into, including stuff he hadn't disclosed to us because it wasn't important information at the time.

Sting's face hardened. "I see."

Warlock sighed, scrubbing a hand over his face as if it were just one more nail in his coffin. "Is that true, Bev? Has all this been some elaborate long con to get information about the club?"

She shrugged. "Conspiracies. Sword obviously got them to believe a lot of things about me, and Chloe is simply helping them buy into me being the bad guy here. They're the ones who've kidnapped my daughter! It's your duty to bring her home!"

Warlock and Chloe looked at each other a long time. Neither said a word, but I got the feeling there was a wealth of communication going on. "I don't think so." Warlock met my gaze again. "You take care of her. She's right. I tried to keep my distance from her, too. But I always watched out for her. It was the only reason I let Bev talk her into coming to the clubhouse to meet Sting. I knew my son would take care of Chloe, too."

"Well, thanks," I said with a little sarcastic sneer. "But you can't have her. She's mine."

Sting raised his hands. "Ain't sayin' it woulda been hard to make her my ol' lady. But if she's happy, I'm not going to take her away from you."

"The hell you're not!" Bev rounded on Sting, crossing in front of Warlock. "You're going to get my daughter and you're going to make her your ol' lady. Then you're going to welcome Warlock back into the family, and we're all going home!"

"That's enough!" Sting dismounted his bike and stomped toward Bev. Instead of backing off, the other woman lunged for him. Too late, I realized what she'd done.

Bev snagged Sting's gun in the holster at his hip. He'd unsnapped the strap securing his weapon for ease of use, and Bev had known he'd prepare. I called out a warning just as Bev took aim at Chloe and fired. I tried to dart in front of her, but something knocked me out of the way in a full-on body tackle. With a roar, Sword flung his body between Bev and Chloe, flattening me in the process. The gun went off just as he hit me. His body jerked with the impact of the bullet, knocking him to his back on the ground. Chloe screamed as several men from Bones surrounded us, all of them pulling their weapons but not firing. They were too well-trained for that. They wouldn't pull the trigger unless Cain gave the order.

Warlock had Bev's gun hand above her head, his other arm around her body, pinning her other arm to her side and her body to his. He looked at Sting, who shook his head slightly, then reached for the gun in Bev's hand, taking it from her. All the while, Bev screamed obscenities at them both.

"I'll make sure you both go to fucking prison! Let me go, you bastard!"

"Stop struggling." Warlock didn't sound winded or strained in the least. "Why would you think you could send us to prison?"

"Because that's my job!" She spat the words. "You don't honestly think I stayed with you all this time because I liked your company, do you? Heaven knows you're not a good fuck. I was tasked with finding out what your stupid club does with the people you hunt down. We know you kill them. That makes you all serial killers!"

"I thought you were looking into Argent Tech." Sword sounded pained and hadn't gotten off the ground, but it was clear he wanted to know what this was all about, too.

"They were. With ExFil. Someone at Argent found out and warned them off or something. I don't know. Don't care. I do what they tell me to."

"They?" Cain took a step toward Bev.

"The feds. CIA. FBI. ATF. Whatever."

"How much are they paying you?" Sting now crossed to stand beside Cain, both men between Bones and Iron Tzars. Bev and Warlock stood between the Tzars and Bones.

At first, Bev refused to say anything. She just stuck her chin up stubbornly. Then Warlock slid his hand up her body to circle her throat, squeezing. I winced and glanced at Chloe who, surprisingly, was beside Sword on the ground, holding pressure to the wound in his shoulder. Her face could have been made from stone.

"How much, Bev?" Warlock's voice could have been a caress had he not started to squeeze the woman's throat like he meant business.

Bev struggled, her free hand going to Warlock's big, muscled arm. "Three thousand a month," she got out. "Three thousand!"

Warlock let up on her, then wrapped his arms back around her, taking her arms with him to pin against her body again. If the situation had been different, it would have looked like he was embracing her instead of restraining her. His face was at her neck as he whispered something into her ear. She shivered, but I didn't think it was with arousal. She suddenly looked terrified.

"She wired?" Cain met Sting's gaze before shifting to Warlock's.

"No." Warlock said, certainty in his voice. "I found all the bugs a few days ago. When we were getting ready for this trip, I handpicked clothing and jewelry for her. She's not wearing anything that hasn't been cleaned." Bev gasped, trying to look back at Warlock but he hushed her, rubbing his cheek against her hair.

"Good." Sting turned to Chloe and walked toward her, shouldering his way carefully between the Bones men. "Chloe, I'm sorry. I should have made it clear to you you'd never be in danger with our club. I should have told you I knew Bev was trying to manipulate us all, but I wasn't sure how much you were in on and didn't want to make assumptions. Not when I was so new in the position of president of a club I grew up in and would give up my last breath for."

"I understand," she said softly. "You had to protect your family."

"Yes, but not at the expense of an innocent. I should have reassured you so you would give me a chance and not run at the first opportunity." He jerked his head in my direction. "You good? Staying with Deadeye?"

"Yes."

"Did some research on him. He's a straight-up killer when he needs to be. Far as I can tell from his service record, he never missed a target he aimed for. Every kill he was ordered to make, he took out. You sure you want to tie yourself to a man like that?"

"Talk like that's gonna land you in my sights." I balled my hands into fists. Sting just chuckled.

"See? Bit hot-headed for a sniper, but I suppose keeping you is more important to him than his control." Sting nodded like he was supremely satisfied with the turn of events.

Chloe smiled. "Yeah. I'm good. He saved me." She looked down at Sword. His face was grimaced in pain, but he said nothing. "Sword saved me too. And Goose, though I've yet to meet him. Maybe he's a bit shy."

"Goose, huh." Sting looked back at me. "Not Major 'Goose' Rio."

That startled me. "As a matter of fact. You know him, then."

"We did a tour together. So yeah." He turned back to Chloe. "You're right. He's not what I'd call an extrovert. Don't worry. He'll have your back even though you don't see him."

Chloe's eyes got wide, and she shifted her gaze to me. "Isaac..." My name was a whisper on her lips.

She looked from me back to Sting.

"What?"

Sword shifted. "Sniper!" His voice was strangled with pain, and he weakly rolled, trying to take Chloe with him.

My gaze snapped to Sting and saw the red dot of a laser on his forehead. It was rock steady at first. Then it moved in a tight circle three times before switching off. "That was Goose. Letting you know he's got your back, baby."

"Motherfucker." Sting chuckled, shaking his head. "Yeah, Chloe. Goose has your back."

"I know I'm still in the doghouse," Sword said from the ground where he was now on his belly and still. The bullet hadn't exited his back, so it was most likely still lodged in his shoulder. "But can someone please get me to Mama and Pops before I bleed out?"

"Not sure you're bleeding that much, bro," I said, chuckling. Surprisingly, Chloe glared back at me.

"The man took a bullet for us, Deadeye." She gave me a cute little scowl as she helped Sword turn over. He groaned as he landed on his back once more. She immediately put pressure back on his wound. Sword groaned and looked up at her with the saddest puppy dog eyes I'd ever seen in my life.

Immediately, Chloe pursed her lips. "Nope. Calling bullshit. You're hurt and, while I'm grateful you took that bullet for me, you're not hurt that bad. I bet you've taken worse."

"That obvious?"

"Dude! You work for a bunch of mercenaries!" Chloe looked put out, but she still held pressure on his wound.

"We're not mercenaries. Exactly." Then his expression changed. "I just wanted some sympathy so maybe you'd accept my apology." This time, he looked sincere. "I really am sorry. I'll regret my actions as long as I live."

Her expression softened. "I understand why you assumed the worst. My mother is a piece of work."

"You'll forgive me, then?"

"Yes. You risked yourself more than once to save my ass. The least I can do is give you another chance." She frowned down at him. "Who beat you up?"

"Your man. A few days ago."

"Oh. Yeah. I knew that." She winced slightly. "Sorry."

"Wasn't your fault, baby. He did what any man in his position would have done. Shoulda done worse."

"Well, it's over now." Chloe stood, backing away from Sword when a couple of the brothers helped him to his feet.

"When did you get here?" Cain approached Sword, and the big man winced at the look on Cain's face.

"Uh, yeah. About that."

"You were told in no uncertain terms to stay in your quarters. Yes?"

"I was."

"And you deliberately disobeyed my orders."

"I did."

Cain sighed heavily. "I'm gettin' too fuckin' old for this shit."

"Please, Cain." Chloe walked up to the older man, laying a hand on his arm. "Don't punish him further. He saved my life. If that bullet had hit me... It got him in the shoulder, but it would have hit my head."

"Yeah. I noticed that, too." Cain gave my

shoulder an awkward pat. "Go to your man. The two of you can deal with Sword until Magenta takes him back." He made eye contact with Sword again. "But you're still on probation."

"Didn't expect anything less."

Cain turned back to the Iron Tzars. "What's the plan for her?" Cain indicated Bev.

Sting shrugged. "About the same thing that would have happened to her if she'd been with your club."

Cain nodded. "'Bout what I thought. You gonna wait till you get home?"

"What are you talking about?" Bev was still held by Warlock. He seemed reluctant to let her go. The man had to know what was coming. Would he fight for her life? I didn't think so. He knew it had to be done. Especially if she was in a ring trying to take down their club. Possibly ours, too.

"You know the penalty for betrayal, Bev." Sting's voice was quiet.

"Go on, Chloe." I tried to express to Sword my need for him to get Chloe out of the area. I knew this was happening now. Cain would insist on it so he could make sure the body was disposed of. Not dropped off somewhere in our territory for law enforcement or some innocent bystander to find. I didn't want Chloe to see this. Thankfully, the man understood.

"I'm kinda woozy."

"You can't ride a bike in this shape."

"Take the side-by-side." Cain nodded to the vehicle he and Daniel had ridden in. Cain had known there might be a need to get rid of a body. Or bodies. He'd come prepared. "Get him to Mama so she can take a look at that wound."

"What's happening?" Chloe looked up at me, her eyes wide with fear.

"Just take care of Sword. He needs you."

"This is one of those things I don't want to know. Isn't it?"

"Yeah, baby." I pulled her to me and kissed the top of her head, holding her close for several seconds before letting her go. "Go on now. I'll come get you when this is done."

For a moment, I didn't think she'd do what I told her. Then she nodded, glancing once at Bev. "Goodbye, Mother." Then she looked at me again and nodded. She helped Sword into the vehicle -- the man really was milking it -- then climbed in herself and took off. Back to the clubhouse.

I turned back to face the Tzars. Sting met my gaze. "I'm glad you sent your woman away."

"She doesn't need to see this."

"See what?" Bev struggled to get away from Warlock, but the man held firm, not saying a word. "You can't do this!"

"You know we can. You know we are." Sting had absolutely no give to him. He checked his gun and chambered a round. "Better to get it over with than to torture you further with the ride home."

"What? Stop it! Let me go!" Bev struggled in earnest now, trying her best to get away from the man at her back.

When Warlock let her go, I thought Sting would shoot her, but Warlock didn't get out of the way. Instead, he turned her around to face him.

"Shh, Bev. Look at me."

"I don't want to look at you, you bastard!"

"But you will. You shared my bed. I gave you everything you ever wanted. Gave you more than I was prepared to give when I met you but did it willingly. The least you can do is look at me now."

The pain in Warlock's eyes made me wince. Bev finally looked up at him. The big man cupped her face gently in his big hands and bent to kiss her. When he lifted his head, he retained his hold on her face, gazing down into her eyes before shifting his hold slightly and wrenching her head hard to the right, snapping her neck.

The second her neck broke, her body collapsed. Warlock caught her and sank to the ground, raising his face to the sky to bellow in pain. He roared, sounding like a wounded animal. That was when I realized the man had truly loved her. I pitied him but knew I couldn't show it.

Sting started slightly. Like he hadn't been expecting Warlock's actions. Then he shook his head once before meeting Cain's stony expression with one of his own. "We can take care of this."

"We'll do it." Cain's reply was soft, respectful of Warlock's pain. "I'll make sure we're gentle with her, out of respect for your father."

"I appreciate that. I'm sorry I brought this to your door, Cain. Bones is on the up and up. I own you one, and I fully intend to repay you." He stuck out his hand to Cain, and our president took it in a solid grip. "You know how to get in touch with us if you need an extra set of hands."

"I do. Same with us. I'd like to form an open dialogue between our clubs. We looked into what the Tzars do and approve. Your business is your own but know that we'd be willing to assist in times of need."

The phrasings were danced around carefully, but the meaning was taken. The Iron Tzars departed, leaving only Warlock holding Bev in his arms.

"She was a bitch," Warlock finally said, still looking at Bev's face. Her eyes were open, and she'd grown pale in death. "But, for some reason, my heart wanted her."

"You can't help that," Cain said. "Sometimes we make fools of ourselves over our women. Hopefully, you'll find yourself a woman worthy of the effort in the future."

"I'm done. Nothing is worth this." He shook his head and stood, Bev securely in his arms.

Daniel brought back the side-by-side, minus Chloe and Sword. He pulled up beside Warlock. The big man gently laid his woman in the back, brushing a lock of her hair off her forehead. Daniel handed him a blanket and Warlock tucked it around her before pulling a tarp over the back to cover the body.

"Fuckin' bitch," he muttered. "I hope you rot in hell."

Chapter Eight
Chloe

I knew my mother was dying as I drove Sword to the clinic where Mama fussed over him appropriately. Especially when she realized I wasn't leaving him to deal with this on his own. The man had taken a bullet for me. Literally fallen on his sword and sacrifice himself to save me. I still had reservations, but I knew I'd be a bitch if I didn't give the man a chance. And, oh, he was milking it.

"My back!" He groaned and winced as I helped him move to the stretcher. "Can you get me a pillow to put under my knees? I think I hurt my back when I landed after jumping in front of you." He gave me a look so filled with pain and sadness, I rolled my eyes, but fluffed the pillow behind his head and found one for his legs, repositioning it several times before he was satisfied. He wasn't mean or grumpy, just... like a hurt puppy. It made me want to love on him until he was quiet and comfortable. When I scowled at him, I saw him fight a grin before he looked up at me like he was helpless as a newborn babe.

"If you try to make that girl feel sorry for you one more time, Sword, I'll give you something for her to really feel sorry for you about."

"Can't a man get a little attention from his daughter without taking criticism?"

"He might. If it was warranted." Mama scrubbed his wound a little more vigorously than I thought was strictly necessary, but at least I knew, this time, his grimace was real. "There. Clean. Now, I need to see if I can get the bullet out." She dug into the wound with a pair of forceps, and Sword gave a sharp yelp before biting down and clenching his jaw.

"Christ, woman! What the fuck?"

Mama didn't look up from her work, just kept digging. "Perhaps if your actions change in the future, should something like this happen again, I'll find a bottle of anesthetic."

Sword grumbled but didn't disagree with her. I caught him looking at me out of the corner of his eye like he thought I would suddenly remember what he'd done and storm out. Finally, I just sighed and sat on a stool next to him. I held out my hand and raised my eyebrow when he just looked at it. Finally, he looked away. But he also took my hand. Blinking rapidly, he grunted and started grumbling at Mama once again. The older woman snipped back at him but gave me a wink when he wasn't looking.

Something inside me settled. Perhaps this was the first step toward healing. Toward getting to know my father. I didn't have answers to questions like that. But I knew it felt right. So, yeah. I'd forgive Sword and start over with him. What happened after that, well. We'd see.

"Chloe?" I turned to find Isaac walking through the door. He came to me and pulled me into his arms. I let go of Sword's hand to another round of grumbling from the big man.

"I need my daughter, Deadeye. Can you see I'm sufferin' here?"

Mama head-slapped him. "Not another word. That girl is getting to know more than just your sorry self."

I ignored the byplay and looked up at Isaac, needing to know what had happened. He enfolded me in his arms and kissed the top of my head, not saying another word. I knew she was dead. It was done.

For long moments I just let him hold me. I

thought tears would come, but they wouldn't. I thought I'd feel... something. Anything. But I didn't. Then I recognized a very unwelcome emotion riding up to engulf me like a big, fuzzy sweater.

Relief. Overwhelming, shaming, *damning* relief.

I turned to Sword to find him looking at me intently. He'd stayed Mama's hand and sat up on the stretcher. It was at that moment I understood how Sword's emotions had gotten the better of him when he'd first seen me. That thought more than anything nearly brought me to tears. It didn't mean he was justified in his actions. It just meant I wasn't any better than he was regarding my feelings. He just took out his feelings on the wrong person.

"I get it," I said. "It doesn't justify your actions, but I get it."

"No, honey. It doesn't. I just hope you can forgive me and let me start over with you." He shook his head. "I don't deserve it, but I'm asking for it anyway. Magenta has given me a son and a daughter. If I'd known Bev was pregnant with you, I'd have done everything in my power to make sure she couldn't use you like she used me. Like she used Warlock."

I nodded. "What was it about her that made people do what she wanted?"

Sword shook his head. "I was only twenty-three, Chloe. She was sophisticated and beautiful. I don't know of any man in my position at the time who could have resisted her. I can't speak for Warlock, but I was just blinded by the all the bling she represented and too stupid to realize I had nothing to offer a woman like her at that time in my life. She was adept at recognizing what men wanted and giving it to them."

"I'm sorry I judged you so harshly. My mother's dead, and all I feel is a nearly overwhelming sense of relief."

"No, Chloe. You feel exactly the way you should. She might have fucked with my head, but she never controlled my actions. That was all on me."

"Thanks for saving my life. Twice."

"Hey, I helped, too." Isaac tugged me toward the door. "And you haven't checked me over. I could have been hurt, too. Big bastard knocked me to the ground. My shoulder hurts and stuff."

Sword scowled. "Take her on, then. I'll just hang out here with Mama until she sews me up. Assuming I survive. Her bedside manner leaves a lot to be desired."

I paused, remembering Magenta had kicked him out of the house. "Go home when you get done. I think you've earned it."

He raised his eyebrows. "Oh yeah?"

"Yeah. You took a bullet for me. I think Magenta will accept you've done your penance." I'd call her and put in a good word for him. I thought she'd give in to my wishes. Sword wasn't a bad man, or a cruel one. If I could forgive him and give him a second chance, I thought she might, too.

Isaac took me to our room. Once inside, he stripped me and put me in the shower with him, washing every inch of my skin before following his hands with his lips.

"I could have lost you tonight. Pretty sure I told you to stay with the women."

"I know. And I'm sorry. But I couldn't let you fight my battles for me. Not by yourself. Besides, I needed a chance to say goodbye."

"I'm so sorry, Chloe. If it helps, it was quick, and she wasn't expecting it."

"Honestly? It doesn't matter. I'm glad I missed

the end, but I needed the closure. What's Warlock going to do?"

"Not sure, honey. He and Cain talked, and he said something about maybe going to Florida and Lake Worth to Black Reign, but he was pretty adamant he'd not get mixed up with another club. He's pretty down on himself over what happened with your mother. Unfortunately for him, El Diablo has taken an interest in him. From what I've seen, El Diablo usually gets what he wants."

"Magenta and Zora both mentioned El Diablo. Is Black Reign a motorcycle club?"

"Yeah. He didn't start it, but he took it over. They're kind of a law unto themselves. Have a hand in the local government of Palm Springs."

"Wherever he goes, I hope he finds peace. He's not a bad man. Just manipulated by a woman I was pretty sure he loved."

"Yeah, baby. He loved your mother. Now, this whole thing is over, I need you. I need to know you're still mine."

I smiled. "I'm all yours, Isaac. Take what you need."

That was the only encouragement he needed. Isaac kissed me like it was the last time he ever would, and I surrendered willingly. I let him sweep me along in a sea of pleasure, his big body wrapping around mine as he continued to kiss me. It was amazing to me what he could do with just his lips, tongue, and teeth, but he did. Every time he kissed me it was this way. My body cried out for his. I needed the pleasure only he could provide.

"Are you wet for me, Chloe?" His fingers already sought the answer to his question before I had the chance to speak.

"You know I am."

"Good." He stroked my clit before turning me around to face the shower wall, lifting one of my legs to rest on the shelf. Then he gripped my hips and slid inside me with a slow, wicked glide.

Every time he entered me, his size stretched me, creating an erotic burn I knew I'd never get tired of feeling. He let me have a few moments to adjust before he started fucking me in long, steady strokes.

"God, you feel good around me, Chloe." His voice shook with the effort he put into our lovemaking. The longer he kept going, the harder he fucked me. "Can't get enough of you, woman!"

"Do it, Deadeye." I hissed the command, calling him by his road name to get his back up. I knew he wanted me to call him by his given name, but sometimes, I thought it was necessary to poke the bear. "Fuck me!"

"Little witch! I'll fuck you, all right!"

Over and over he plunged into me. Our mingled cries echoed in the bathroom as the hot water rained down on us. I reached for my orgasm, but it wouldn't come. Not in this position. Isaac seemed to know what I needed because one arm snaked around me and found my clit hidden between my folds and stroked. The second he touched me, I came, clamping down on his dick so hard it actually hurt. There wasn't enough room inside me for him. Especially when he started to swell, his own orgasm nearing.

"Fuck, Chloe! Fuckin' little cunt's squeezin' my cum from me! AHH!"

His seed exploded hotly inside me. His arms locked around me, holding me tightly to him, my back to his front. Had he not held me up, I was sure I'd have fallen to the shower floor. Instead, he took my weight and kissed the side of my neck, praising my responses to him.

"So fuckin' beautiful, baby. Love that look on your face when you let go and come all over my dick. Fuckin' love it."

"Isaac..." My sigh was barely above a whisper. There was so much I needed to tell him. So much I was feeling inside. I just didn't know how to voice it. Did I love him? I wasn't sure. I thought I might.

"I've got you, baby. I've got you."

He turned off the water and lifted me into his arms, setting me on the vanity before drying me off. Then he dried himself, standing with his hips between my legs so I could lean on him. I kissed his shoulder and chest until he finished, then he wrapped his arms around me, my legs around his waist, and carried me to the bed.

Once he'd settled us, I sighed contentedly, snuggling against him with my head on his shoulder.

"You're a phenomenal woman, Chloe. I'm one lucky bastard to have you with me."

"I'm the lucky one. Thanks for taking me in. For giving a damn about me."

He was silent for a long moment, then he swore softly. "I ain't good at this, so I'm just gonna say it." He took a breath. "I love you, Chloe. Ain't sure when it happened, and you don't have to say it back. I just want you to know."

I sucked in a breath and pushed up so I could look down at him. "Don't say that if you don't mean it. I can take it if you don't -- but I can't believe you love me, then have you take it back."

"Don't say shit I don't mean. Especially not with you. You're my one and only, Chloe. My woman."

I giggled through the tears that suddenly sprang

to my eyes. "I love you, too. You're the most amazing man I've ever met."

"I'll have your property patch in a couple of days, then we'll make it official. I've already claimed you, but the cut will show everyone in this club or any other that you're under my protection. My ol' lady."

"I don't care about anyone else. As long as you know I'm yours, that's all that matters to me."

"Well, I know it, baby. You're mine and I'm yours."

With a contented sigh, I lay back against his body. "I think you're the miracle I never thought I'd have, Isaac."

"Not me, baby. That's you. The miracle is all you."

Marteeka Karland

Erotic romance author by night, emergency room tech/clerk by day, Marteeka Karland works really hard to drive everyone in her life completely and totally nuts. She has been creating stories from her warped imagination since she was in the third grade. Her love of writing blossomed throughout her teenage years until it developed into the totally unorthodox and irreverent style her English teachers tried so hard to rid her of.

Bones MC Multiverse:
- Bones MC
- Salvation's Bane MC
- Shadow Demons
- Black Reign MC
- Iron Tzars MC

Marteeka at Changeling: changelingpress.com/marteeka-karland-a-39

Changeling Press E-Books

More Sci-Fi, Fantasy, Paranormal, and BDSM adventures available in e-book format for immediate download at ChangelingPress.com -- Werewolves, Vampires, Dragons, Shapeshifters and more -- Erotic Tales from the edge of your imagination.

What are E-Books?

E-books, or electronic books, are books designed to be read in digital format -- on your desktop or laptop computer, notebook, tablet, Smart Phone, or any electronic e-book reader.

Where can I get Changeling Press E-Books?

Changeling Press e-books are available at ChangelingPress.com, Amazon, Apple Books, Barnes & Noble, and Kobo/Walmart.

ChangelingPress.com

Printed in Great Britain
by Amazon